SNOWED IN WITH A COLTON

Lisa Childs

HARLEQUIN

ROMANTIC
SUSPENSE

Special thanks and acknowledgment are given to Lisa Childs for her contribution to The Coltons of Colorado miniseries.

HARLEQUIN®
ROMANTIC SUSPENSE™

Recycling programs
for this product may
not exist in your area.

ISBN-13: 978-1-335-75961-0

Snowed In With a Colton

Copyright © 2022 by Harlequin Books S.A.

This edition published by arrangement with Harlequin Books S.A.

For questions and comments about the quality of this book, please contact us at CustomerService@Harlequin.com.

Harlequin Enterprises ULC
22 Adelaide St. West, 41st Floor
Toronto, Ontario M5H 4E3, Canada
www.Harlequin.com

Printed in U.S.A.

Ever since **Lisa Childs** read her first romance novel (a Harlequin story, of course) at age eleven, all she wanted was to be a romance writer. With over seventy novels published with Harlequin, Lisa is living her dream. She is an award-winning, bestselling romance author. She loves to hear from readers, who can contact her on Facebook or through her website, lisachilds.com.

Books by Lisa Childs

Harlequin Romantic Suspense

The Coltons of Colorado

Snowed In With a Colton

Bachelor Bodyguards

Bodyguard's Baby Surprise
Beauty and the Bodyguard
Nanny Bodyguard
Single Mom's Bodyguard
In the Bodyguard's Arms
Soldier Bodyguard
Guarding His Witness
Evidence of Attraction
Boyfriend Bodyguard
Close Quarters with the Bodyguard

Visit the Author Profile page at Harlequin.com for more titles.

With great appreciation for the
Harlequin Romantic Suspense editorial team:
Patience Bloom, Carly Silver and Megan Broderick.

Prologue

The heat of the fire warmed his skin, making the hairs on his forearms tingle. The acrid smoke filled his nostrils, and his lungs began to burn.

The building's windows were all aglow from the flames burning within, and he was standing too close to it, in an alley behind, which hadn't been blocked off by the emergency crews already on-site. The firefighters were working to extinguish the fire and to make sure everybody got out.

He, too, had to make sure that everybody was safe, that nobody suffered because of him. Because this was his fault.

He hadn't set this fire, hadn't started the hotel burning, but every place he'd stayed had had some malfunction— something that led to a fire. To devastation…

But not to what it was supposed to have led to…

His death.

That was what this fire was meant to have caused. When was the Camorra going to give up its quest for revenge? His exposé had led to several arrests—of people within their organization as well as of people in governments and legal authorities that had helped them conduct their business.

Those arrests should have weakened the Camorra in Naples, but enough of them must have remained free. Or maybe they were conducting their business yet from behind bars.

He knew they would not be done with him until he was dead. They would keep trying, keep tracking him down, as they had at every place he'd hidden.

Was there any place he could go where he'd finally be safe—where other people's lives wouldn't be put at risk just for being near him?

Chapter 1

The Truth Foundation.

Because the truth was very important to her family, Aubrey Colton loved its name. After all, her dad had used his power as a judge to send innocent people to jail and take kickbacks—and she was determined to be nothing like that. To atone for his misdeeds, her siblings had formed the organization to help wrongly convicted people fight for exoneration or get reduced sentences for criminals who had gotten overly harsh ones because of the not-so-honorable Benjamin Colton. While she supported the idea that no innocent person should be left in prison, she worried about accidentally freeing someone who was actually culpable, though. Too many of the guilty claimed innocence.

Like her slimy ex-boyfriend…

Her cell phone, in the pocket of her flannel shirt, vibrated against her breast. She'd shut off the ringer while she and her twin, Jasper, had been at a meeting held in the downtown Blue Larkspur offices of Colton & Colton. That was where the law practice of her oldest siblings, twins Caleb and Morgan, was situated. She was glad now that she hadn't turned her ringer back on, as she was able to ignore her cell and focus on driving.

She and Jasper had peaced out of the meeting early, using the excuse that they had work to do at Gemini Ranch, the dude ranch they co-owned. Usually they were too busy with work to help out much with the foundation. But fortunately there were twelve of them, including her, so the workload was spread around.

"Are you okay?" Jasper asked.

Aubrey glanced away from the road to her twin, who sat in the passenger seat of the truck she drove. They didn't look exactly like each other. His hair was more strawberry blond than her lighter locks, but they had the same dark blue eyes. He didn't have to wear glasses like she did, though. "Why do you ask?"

"Well, for someone who cares so much about being truthful, you didn't mind stretching it to get out of that meeting." He grinned. "We're *so busy* at the ranch right now…" He mimicked her voice, repeating what she'd told their siblings just moments ago.

"Well, we are," she insisted self-righteously, her face heating a little over being called out. That was why their partnership worked so well: they never had hesitated to call each other on their crap. Jasper knew her so well; he was aware she wasn't as interested in the foundation as their siblings were. While she appreciated its intent, she was too worried that someone guilty might get set free and hurt someone else. She didn't want to be even partially responsible for that happening.

He snorted. "It's March. The cattle drives aren't happening right now, so we only have a handful of rooms booked."

Their working dude ranch was of course busier in the warmer months. But in the winter, guests could still enjoy horseback riding—either outside or in the indoor ring—and there was snowshoeing, skiing and snowmobiling to do as well. And when they came in from the cold, they especially appreciated the spa facilities and hot tubs and the mammoth fireplace in the main lodge.

The ranch was her main concern; they'd dreamed about starting it for so long and had worked so hard to have their dream realized that she wanted to make sure it thrived. "More guests are checking in, so of course, we need to make sure everything's ready. And," she reminded him, "you've been yammering on about some snowstorm in the long-range forecast that's going to hit the area hard."

But she wasn't so sure. The streets of Blue Larkspur, Colorado, were clear and dry now. And the grass was beginning to turn from brown to green as it bathed in the sunlight. That sunlight glinted off the Colorado River that bordered town and made the roads twist and wind as she headed toward the nearby mountains. Snow clung yet to the peaks, the temperature still too low at those elevations to melt it away. Gemini Ranch was located between the city and those mountains.

"A storm is coming," Jasper insisted. "It's going to hit later this week, so we do need to get the cattle moved in closer."

They were drawing closer now, driving along the fence that marked the roadside of their one-hundred-acre property. Sometime over the next few days, she and Jasper would move the cattle to these pastures to make sure they got food and water in case the storm raged on for as long as Jasper seemed to believe it would.

"See, then we do have a lot of work to do at the ranch," she said in her defense. "I wasn't stretching the truth at all—which is probably more than Ronald Spence can say..."

"You don't think the Truth Foundation should take his case?" Jasper asked.

Ronald Spence was currently serving several life sentences for the crimes he'd committed as the head of a drug smuggling ring. But six months ago he'd started claiming that he was wrongly convicted, that there was evidence out there to clear him and prove that he had been the operation's fall guy.

Aubrey didn't easily believe anyone anymore, so she just shrugged. "I don't know..."

"This could be the last one, you know..." Jasper murmured.

"The last one of the rulings that Dad was paid to deliver..." She cringed at the knowledge of what their dad had done, how he'd forfeited justice for money. As a judge, he'd accepted bribes from private prisons and juvenile detention centers to deliver tougher sentences to offenders.

But would he have let someone guilty go free while knowingly sending someone else to jail for that person's crimes?

She shuddered at the thought. Usually, she tried not

to think about the Colton family's past and their father's legacy of corruption. She focused on Gemini Ranch and making that her legacy. Hers and her twin's. That was why it was so important to her—to them. She wanted to provide wonderful memories for her guests to carry home with them from their stay at the working dude ranch. She wanted families to bond there and couples to reconnect or for singles to find the solace and comfort they sought.

Jasper uttered a weary-sounding sigh. "It's sad…"

It was more than sad. It was *tragic*.

Just like their dad's death in a car accident before he'd gone on trial for his corruption. His victims had never gotten true justice. So if Ronald Spence was being honest…

She sighed, too, as she slowed the truck for the turn into the long driveway. "I know the foundation needs to investigate, needs to make certain…" *that Ronald Spence had not been another victim of their father's greed and corruption.*

"Caleb and Morgan will figure out if Spence is innocent," Jasper assured her.

But she shook her head. "How does anyone really know if someone's actually telling the truth?" she wondered. "Look at how Dad fooled Mom all those years, making her think that his money beyond his salary came from a family inheritance."

"Is it just Dad who's made you distrust everyone?" Jasper asked. "Or is it that idiot Warren Parker?"

She nearly shuddered again at her twin's mention of her ex-boyfriend. But she didn't know if she blamed Warren for lying to her or herself for falling for those lies.

She should have known better, especially after what her father had done to her mother—to all of them. How had she missed all the red flags of another man's falsehoods?

Or had she seen and just ignored them because she'd wanted to believe that someone loved her after she'd finally opened up to a man?

As it turned out, the only thing Warren had been attracted to was the money he'd thought she made as half owner of the ranch, and he'd needed that money for his gambling debts. He hadn't gotten anything out of Aubrey. Even though she'd fallen for some of his lies, she hadn't fallen irretrievably head over heels for him. When he'd verbally lashed out at her after she refused to pay his debts and had admitted that he was only after money, she'd been hurt but nothing like Dad had hurt Mom. Nothing like that…

And she would make certain that she was never hurt like that. Even all these years after Ben Colton's death, Isadora Colton was still struggling with the devastation of his lies. They all were, in their own ways—even her, with her reluctance to trust or fall in love. All Warren Parker had done was confirm what she already knew; she was better off single than being with someone she couldn't trust. No. She wasn't just better off. She was better—happier.

"Aubrey," Jasper prodded her, "you're not going to let that loser Warren keep you from dating anyone else, are you?"

She snorted. "Of course not." And she wouldn't let Warren or even her father keep her from falling for a good man. That is, if one, besides her brothers, actually existed. "But the next person I date will have to be so transparent that I can see right through him. No lies. No deceptions. No secrets."

Luca Rossi knew his life had become a complete lie. He wasn't sure when he would ever be able to tell the truth again. Or *if* he would ever be able to tell the truth again…

If he was honest with anyone, he would be putting them in danger, too. The same threat that had followed him to nearly every place he had hidden since he had reported the crimes of the Camorra in his native Naples.

Maybe it just wasn't possible to hide from the Camorra since the gangsters kept finding him everywhere he'd gone.

Or at least that was what he believed, but maybe he was just paranoid. Maybe all those things that had happened were just accidents…

And not the Italian criminal organization's attempts on his life. First there had been that fire at the B and B in Toronto and then another fire at the hotel in Wisconsin, and that car that had nearly run him down in the street in Iowa…

Those could have been accidents, coincidences. But he doubted it and because he didn't want anyone else to get hurt, he couldn't risk it. He couldn't risk staying in one place for too long or getting too close to anyone.

Constantly moving, constantly traveling, was how Luca had wound up here in Blue Larkspur, Colorado, on Gemini Ranch. But here he wasn't Luca Rossi; now he was Luke Bishop.

Luke Bishop had checked into a private cabin at

Gemini Ranch—one far enough away from the main lodge and the other cabins that nobody else would get hurt if he was found yet again. On a travel blog, he'd read about the working dude ranch and had figured since it was the off season, there would be few other guests or even employees for him to endanger if the Camorra tracked him down.

In the week since Luke Bishop had arrived there, nobody had seemed to notice him much at all. He hadn't felt as he had in other places, as if he was being watched. Maybe he'd finally lost whoever had tailed him from his home in Naples.

Maybe he was finally safe.

But as safe as he was, he was getting bored. His restlessness must have affected the horse he was riding, which lurched forward. Enjoying the exhilaration of the sudden rush of speed, Luca urged the dark bay gelding to go faster.

They raced against the wind, which riffled through Luca's hair and chafed his skin. He didn't care; he raised his face to it, breathing in the fresh air and the sunshine.

Colorado—and the Gemini Ranch especially—were beautiful. Luca should have been at peace there, but that restlessness persisted. Boredom…

He'd never done well with it. As a boy, he'd gotten in trouble in school whenever he was bored. And as a man, he'd found that it compelled him to take risks that other people didn't dare to take…

Like going undercover as a Camorrista to find incriminating evidence against the gangsters to write that exposé about the Camorra for a local political newspaper—an article that had gone viral and led to numerous convictions and arrests. But apparently not enough. Not enough that he was safe yet. Still, he didn't regret what he'd done. He hadn't been able to do what everyone else had been doing, turning a blind eye to crime, to the cold-blooded murders, to the terror with which the Camorra had ruled and ruined so many lives. Instead of living in fear, like so many others in his hometown, he'd taken action. And just as he'd learned as a bored, little kid, there were consequences for actions. His had been living under protection, locked up in windowless rooms, or going on the run. He'd chosen to take his chances on his own—like he always had.

As they neared the barn, the gelding automatically slowed his pace—as if the horse was as reluctant to end their ride as Luca was. Maybe he would go back out and explore the beautiful property some more…

But then he noticed the truck, with the name Gemini Ranch imprinted on the passenger-side door, pulling up near the barn. If new people had been arriving, he would have turned around then, but the name on the door assured him that the vehicle's occupants were workers or the ranch owners. A man pushed open the passenger door. Jasper Colton. The tall blond man was one of the owners of the property; Luca had met him when he'd checked in and then he'd run into him at the barn a few times. Luca hadn't actually met the other owner yet.

He was curious about her because Luca was curious about everyone. He slowed the horse and watched, as he was always people-watching, wondering about their lives…

His curiosity and desire to help people was what had led to all his revelations and all the evidence he'd

unearthed about the Camorra. He'd wanted to end the
reign of terror, had wanted to save lives and have people
feel secure again in their own homes and on the streets
of their city. But surely his interest in the ranch and
its owners wouldn't put him or anyone else in danger?

Then she stepped out of the driver's side and came
around to the box of the truck. Aubrey Colton, he'd
learned her name from the travel blog.

The wind blew through her long blond hair, swirling
it around her face and shoulders. She was so beautiful
and so strong. She lowered the tailgate of the pickup
and pulled out a big bag of something, slinging it over
her shoulder as effortlessly as her brother did.

Aubrey wasn't as tall as her brother, but she was
probably five eight or nine, tall for a woman. And she
was definitely all woman, with voluptuous curves Luca
couldn't help but notice. As she leaned into the bed of
the pickup truck, her jeans stretched taut across her butt.

That restlessness coursed through Luca again, making him want things he had no business wanting. Making him want…

Aubrey.

The horse must have sensed his restlessness again,
because the gelding pawed at the ground and whinnied.
Aubrey glanced back at him and something jolted his
body—a sudden awareness, an attraction—that passed
between them. But then she turned away again, as if
she hadn't been affected at all. Luca realized that in
his boredom he must have been letting his imagination run as wild as the horse had just run on their return to the barn.

Aubrey continued working with her brother, unloading the truck as if she hadn't even noticed him. And she probably hadn't…

She was a busy woman, according to the blog. A no-nonsense businesswoman who probably had no time for dalliances—not with a ranch to run.

Not that Luca wanted to dally with her. He knew he couldn't act on any attraction. Because there was a hit on his life, with people trying to track him down, being anywhere near him would put her in danger, too. Most of his own family had had to flee Naples and live under assumed names, too, for their own safety. And he'd rather sacrifice his own life before he put anyone else in peril.

Where the hell was Luca?

And how the hell did he keep escaping death? Over and over, city after city, he slipped safely away—completely unscathed.

Unlike those he'd left behind in Naples…

Unlike *him*…

If Luca didn't call…

Just then his cell vibrated against the mahogany surface of his desk. The screen lit up with private caller. He tensed as fear and dread gripped him. Was it them?

Were they calling to threaten him again?

Or was it him? Luca kept switching phones just as he kept switching hiding places.

He accepted the call with a hopeful "Ciao?"

"Paolo," a deep voice greeted him.

"Luca?"

"Yes…"

"I've been so worried about you," Paolo said. "Everyone has…"

Luca sighed. "I know. I hate this. I don't want Mama and the others to worry."

Paolo knew that was why his cousin called to check in despite the danger—because he loved his family, but his love for them was going to cost him his life. Paolo ignored the pang of guilt that struck his heart.

He had no choice.

He had to…

Luca could go on the run, could hide out with the money he'd made on all his exposés, on the book he'd been contracted to write.

The only money Paolo had he'd borrowed from the very people who were using those debts and threats to get him to turn his cousin over to them.

"Let me assure her that you're okay," Paolo said. "Where are you? Are you safe? Can she call you on this number?"

Luca chuckled. "Slow down, *cugino*. I cannot tell you where I am—for your safety."

Paolo nearly snorted at the irony of Luca thinking that, which was exactly the opposite. But he couldn't explain that to Luca; the man was too honorable and selfless to understand.

"And Mama cannot call me. I will discard this phone as I've done all the others I've called you from, in case someone's tracking your phone line."

Paolo swallowed a curse. He was the someone tracking his phone line, with an app on his own phone that was trying right now to narrow down Luca's location. He glanced at his screen, at the little light flickering in North America. It needed more time. *He* needed more time.

"At least assure me that you're well," Paolo said. "So that I can tell Aunt Teresa. Are you really all right? You don't sound quite like yourself."

The line went silent, so silent that Paolo was worried that his cousin had hung up, but the light still flickered on the app on his cell screen. Luca hadn't hung up. Why was he so quiet? "Is everything all right?"

"Yes, yes," Luca said. "I'm just bored, I guess. Restless…"

"You want to come home," his cousin surmised.

Luca's weary sigh rattled the phone. "We both know that's not possible."

It was, but Luca would be coming home in a casket. That twinge of guilt struck Paolo again, but he had no choice. He had to…

"So what have you been doing to keep busy?" Paolo asked and hoped like hell that it wasn't writing that book. Luca had done enough damage.

Luca chuckled. "I've been riding."

"Horses?" Paolo asked. But he shouldn't have been surprised; his cousin had once wanted to be a cowboy and had taken riding lessons and had even worked some summers on a cattle ranch. "Are you working on a ranch again?"

Luca sighed again. "I wish. It's a dude ranch that only offers cattle drives when the weather's warm."

"It's not warm there?"

"Not yet," Luca said. "But I better not tell you any more."

"Is that why you don't sound like yourself?" Paolo asked. "Or is it possible that you've met someone?"

There was that hesitation again, and then a repeat of Luca's sigh rattling the cell phone. "No. I haven't met her..."

But there was someone who'd caught his attention, hopefully enough to keep Luca wherever he was until the Camorra could take care of him. And maybe this time, Luca would be too distracted to escape.

The app pinged, and Luca asked, "What was that? I bet someone is tapping the line. I better go. Ciao."

The line clicked off. But it was too late. Paulo had his location, or at least the location of the cell tower through which Luca's call had been placed. That tower was somewhere called Blue Larkspur, Colorado. Now it would be up to the Camorra to find the dude ranch where Luca was hiding. It wouldn't be long now. It would all be over. Paulo rubbed his chest, which ached from the twinge of guilt and loss that *had* struck him. But he had no choice. His cousin had crossed the Camorra; his cousin had to die.

Chapter 2

The morning after the meeting of the Truth Foundation, Aubrey knew where to find Jasper: in the barn. It was where she preferred to be herself, but she'd been busy helping the staff give guests riding lessons in the indoor ring. Not that she minded. This time of year was usually easy for them, more relaxing than the summers, when they were fully booked without a moment to themselves, especially during the cattle drives.

Unfortunately, Jasper was right and that storm was coming. She hopped out of the driver's side of the truck and headed into the barn. After her busy morning with the guests, many of them being young and very loud children, Aubrey took a moment to appreciate the relative silence of the barn and to breathe in the scent of fresh hay.

The barn wasn't entirely silent. The horses shifted

and nickered in their stalls, and the blades of shovels scraped against cement as piles of shavings were mucked out.

Jasper worked in one stall while their one female ranch hand, Kayla St. James, worked in the next. Despite their proximity, they didn't acknowledge each other, didn't speak, which reminded Aubrey of her own strange encounter the day before with their mysterious guest, Luke Bishop.

She shivered now as she remembered how their gazes had locked across the distance between the back of the truck and where he'd ridden up close but not entirely to the barn, as if he'd been holding himself back.

Keeping his distance…

But for that moment, when their eyes had met, that distance had disappeared. She'd felt like she was in his arms, clasped against him.

And her heart had raced, and her breath had caught in her throat. For a minute, she'd wanted things she'd had no business wanting.

Him…

And she didn't even know him. She only knew that he was good-looking. Tall and lean, black hair with a tiny bit of gray in the temples and on the scruff that clung to his angular jaw. His whole face consisted of interesting angles and planes, making him look rugged and yet…

There was more to him than that—something smart and sexy and secretive. She suspected there was more depth to Luke Bishop than he wanted anyone to know.

Because despite all the open rooms in the main lodge, the receptionist had told her that he'd specifically requested a private cabin—the farthest one from the main lodge and from the other guests. He really wanted to be alone. He didn't come to the lodge for meals or social events like the wine tastings or live music. And while Jasper had mentioned meeting and talking with him over the past week that Bishop had been staying at the ranch, Aubrey herself had yet to exchange a word with him.

All she'd exchanged was that *look*…

She shivered again as she remembered and relived the intensity of it, of *him*…and of what she'd felt in that moment. Such a powerful attraction…

"Is it getting cold out?" Jasper asked—with that twin thing where it was almost as if he'd felt the same shiver she had. He stepped out with another shovelful, and when he dumped it into the wheelbarrow between the stalls, Kayla dumped in her load and their shovels clanged.

They didn't even exchange a glance, though. Kayla offered Aubrey a small smile before she stepped back into the stall she'd been cleaning and resumed her work.

Jasper leaned against the open door of the stall he was cleaning. "The first sign the storm's coming is the drop in temperature. That's the cold front moving in."

Aubrey sighed. "You were right. I've heard the reports, too. It sounds like it's going to be bad."

Jasper nodded. "I know. We need to move the cattle from the pastures that are too close to the mountains."

That was for the safety of the livestock and of the hands responsible for taking care of them. If the ranch got the snow and wind that were being predicted, there could be whiteout conditions and even avalanches in the nearby mountains.

She shivered again.

"Must be getting cold," Jasper remarked.

One of the barn doors had opened, but it wasn't so much the cold wind that blew through it but the man who stepped inside the barn that had Aubrey shivering again.

Luke Bishop…

He walked in, leading the gelding he'd been riding yesterday. Wearing a black cowboy hat, a sheepskin-lined denim jacket, jeans and battered-seeming boots, he looked like one of the ranch hands. But guests often dressed as if they were cowboys, too, especially for the cattle drives.

Cattle drives were only scheduled for warmer months of the year, not the colder ones. They ran the ranch with less help in the winter, and usually it wasn't a problem.

Before she could meet his gaze again, Aubrey quickly looked away from their guest and turned back toward her brother. "Do you think we can get any of the family to help us out?" she wondered aloud. "Since we lost one of our best ranch hands when Bruce retired, we're going to need more hands to bring in the cattle, especially since some have just given birth." They would have to go slow, make sure that the mamas and babies didn't get separated.

Jasper shook his head. "I don't know. Everybody's so damn busy—with their own careers and now with this latest Truth Foundation case for Ronald Spence."

"The storm's still a couple of days away from hitting us," Aubrey said. "So we have time to call them, see if we can recruit them or any of our summer staff if they happen to be home—"

"I will help," a deep voice murmured.

Just the sound of his voice had something stirring inside Aubrey, fluttering through her stomach. It was Luke
Bishop. His accent must be French, or maybe Italian...

She glanced back at where he'd walked up behind
her. He was closer now so she could see his eyes. They
were a pale blue with such a riveting gaze that she
caught herself staring just like she'd stared at him yesterday. Those eyes shone with intelligence, but he had
a toughness to him as well. With his skin chafed from
the cold and his lean muscles taut against his jeans and
the sleeves of his jacket, he looked like he was capable
of physical work. Like an artist forced into manual labor
so that he didn't starve...

Aubrey shook her head, clearing away her fanciful
thoughts. She wasn't like that; she didn't romanticize
men. She knew them too well, knew that they lied and
let down the people who loved them most.

"No," she said shortly, before turning back to her
brother.

"But the storm is coming," Jasper said. "We need help."

Aubrey felt as if the storm was inside her with her
tension building. The pressure between two fronts,
warm and cold, shifting everything...

Bringing with it something bad and not just snow
and cold. Something even more unsettling.

Something like their mysterious guest, Luke Bishop.

Luca wasn't used to being so summarily dismissed
as Aubrey Colton had just done, with a glance and a
single word.

No.

As a journalist, he was accustomed to hearing that

word, of course. People often turned down requests for
interviews or for more information. But women didn't
often turn him down, not that he'd often asked them for
anything. He'd been so busy with work over the years
that he hadn't had much time to pursue relationships.
He was usually pursuing a story instead.

Even as bored as he currently was, he didn't have
time for a relationship now, either. Because this would
be the worst possible time for him to get involved with
anyone.

But he couldn't help thinking about Paolo's question the night before, asking if he'd met someone. Not
that he'd actually met Aubrey Colton. They hadn't been
introduced. He only knew, from his research before
checking in, that she was one of the two owners of
Gemini Ranch.

Her brother was the other, so Luca appealed to Jasper
Colton. "I would like to help move the cattle," he said.
"I have worked on other ranches before. I know what
I'm doing." But he wasn't entirely sure about that now.
He was supposed to be keeping his distance; that was
why he'd wanted the private cabin far from the main
lodge and every other cabin. His intention was to not
get too close to anyone, so that he didn't put anyone else
in the danger he was in.

"No," Aubrey repeated, answering before her brother
could. "It's too much of a liability to have a guest help
out."

"But you advertise cattle drives—"

"In the warmer months," she said, interrupting him.
"The storm that's coming in will make the conditions

too dangerous." She spared him another brief, dismissive glance.

And he couldn't help but wonder if she was talking about the storm or him.

Did she somehow sense the threat his very existence posed?

But did it?

How would anyone find him here?

How would they think to look?

How had they thought to find him in any of those other places, though? It was almost as if…

He shook his head now, dismissing that thought before he even allowed it to form. "I've seen the weather reports as well." There was Wi-Fi in the cabin, and he was often online. He didn't have much else to occupy his time…besides the book. "The storm is still a couple of days away. If we move quickly," he said, "we can beat the worst of the snow and win. There will be no danger."

"There is always danger," Aubrey insisted. "Unforeseen threats. Coyotes. Mountain lions. Rattlesnakes…" Her eyes, such a dark and fathomless blue, narrowed behind the lenses of her black-framed glasses as she stared at him.

Did she consider him a snake? Or all men?

"These are the same threats that would be here in the summer," he said. "They are probably bigger threats in the summer, but yet you let guests participate in the cattle drives. In fact, you even charge them more." A grin tugged at his lips, but he only allowed them to curve slightly. "I will pay more if you insist…"

Jasper chuckled. "He's got you, Aub."

She glared at her brother now. "You're the one who's

been harping about this storm," she reminded him. "You know it's too dangerous. We need experienced ranch hands—"

As she had interrupted him, he interrupted her now. "I am experienced..." He lowered his voice on that last word. He couldn't resist teasing her, flirting with her, especially because she was so clearly uninterested.

But she shivered slightly, and he wondered...maybe she was more interested than she wanted to be.

Maybe that was the danger of which she spoke.

She shook her head. "You're not experienced here, at Gemini Ranch. I'm going to bring in hands who know the property, who won't get lost in whiteout conditions, whom we won't have to look for if they go missing."

Thinking of how easily he'd been tracked down over the past several months, Luca murmured, "I am surprisingly easy to find..."

And now he was the one who nearly shivered with fear. Not just for himself, for his safety, but for anyone to whom he got close.

No. Aubrey was right to turn him down. She was smart, smarter than he had been when he'd made the offer to help.

"But I respect your decision," he said, and he respected her more for making it. He touched the brim of his hat, tipping it toward her, before continuing to lead the horse to its empty stall.

The gelding pulled slightly on its reins, as if reluctant to go back. He was restless like Luca, or maybe he only sensed his rider's disquiet.

Luca was more than restless, though. He was intrigued with Aubrey Colton. And he couldn't ever remember a woman arousing his curiosity so much before. A story, certainly, but he suspected that Aubrey had a story of her own, one that had made her smarter and stronger and certainly more distrustful because of it, of whatever had happened in her past.

Jasper watched Aubrey walk off in one direction and Luke Bishop in another, and frustration tugged at him. She was never going to trust anyone again. Not after what Dad had done and certainly not after that loser Warren Parker.

Did she even trust him anymore?

He'd been telling her about the storm, but she hadn't believed him until more reports had come out warning about the danger. She'd certainly had no problem spouting off about that danger and others to Luke Bishop when she'd shot down his offer.

When she'd shot him down as if the guy had been hitting on her. Jasper glanced back at the guest, who disappeared into a stall with Ebony, the gelding. Had he been hitting on Aubrey?

Hell, maybe Jasper had been out of the dating game so long himself that he had missed the signs of flirting, of attraction.

Kayla stepped out of the stall she'd been cleaning then. She didn't even glance at him as she dumped her shovelful of soiled shavings and straw into the wheelbarrow before stepping back inside the stall.

With a sigh, Jasper headed after his sister. She stopped outside the barn, standing next to the pickup as she glanced down at her cell phone.

Had she already sent out the text to their siblings to

request their help? But when he peered over her shoulder at her phone, he noticed it was an incoming text—from Warren Parker.

Give me another chance...

"You haven't blocked that creep?" Jasper asked, appalled that she would have any contact with the man after what he'd done, after how he'd tried to manipulate her into paying off his gambling debts.

Aubrey's face flushed, but that could have been as much from the cold wind blowing as embarrassment. "Reading over my shoulder like when we were kids?" she asked him with exasperation.

He grinned. "It's easier now that I'm taller than you," he said. "And we're twins. We're not supposed to have any secrets."

"We don't," she said. And she swiped her finger across the screen of her cell, deleting Warren's text.

"Then what's your beef with Bishop?" he asked.

She shrugged. "I don't know what you mean. I don't have a beef with him. It's exactly what I said. We can't risk losing a guest during a snowstorm with possible whiteout conditions."

"We won't lose him," Jasper said. "He's been out riding every day since he checked in. He knows the property, and he's a natural in the saddle. I believe that he has experience working some other ranches."

Her face flushed a little deeper red. And Jasper wondered if the two had been flirting in front of him and he'd missed it. No. It would have been Bishop flirting and Aubrey ignoring him.

If only she had ignored Warren when the guy had lavished compliments on her, then maybe she wouldn't be struggling so hard to trust anyone right now. Even him...

"Come on, Aubrey," he urged her. "Give the guy a chance."

"Wh-what do you mean?" she sputtered, and her face definitely got a darker red.

And Jasper wondered...

Was his sister interested in their solitary guest?

"I mean that we have more guests checking in, some couples and another family," he reminded her. "We can't spare any of our already lean crew of staff to help bring in the cattle from—"

"I know," she agreed. "As great as Kayla is as a ranch hand, she's better at giving riding lessons to the guests."

Jasper didn't want Kayla out in the storm anyway, even if she wasn't going to be busy with the guests. He didn't want her getting hurt any more than she already had been. He and Aubrey weren't the only ones at Gemini Ranch who struggled to deal with the sins of their father...

"That's why I'm going to reach out to family," Aubrey said. With as much time as their siblings spent at the ranch, they knew it well.

But Jasper persisted, "Bishop is here. He can help right away."

"He's not leaving?" she asked, with some odd note in her voice.

Like she hoped that he was...

Jasper shook his head. "His stay is open-ended right now. I think he intends to be here for a while."

"Why?" Aubrey asked.

Jasper shrugged. "I don't know. I don't interrogate our guests."

"Maybe we should," she murmured.

"He offered to help," Jasper said. "And thanks to you, he knows every possible danger. He won't be a liability."

Aubrey sighed. "Maybe he won't be a liability…"

"But?" he prodded.

She shrugged now. "I don't know. I just get an odd feeling from the guy…"

Maybe Aubrey hadn't recognized his flirting, either. "Like what?" Jasper asked.

"Like something's going on with him, like he might *be* the danger…" She shivered, and Jasper suspected it had nothing to do with the cold.

"How? Why?" he asked. And he was glad that he wasn't so cynical, that he didn't struggle as hard as she did to trust anyone.

She shook her head. "I don't know…"

"Then give him a chance," Jasper urged.

"I have a feeling that if I do, we'll both come to regret it," Aubrey warned him.

Both—did she mean her and Jasper? Or her and Luke Bishop?

Before he could ask, she was pulling open the driver's door of the truck and hopping inside, and for once the twin intuition didn't work. He didn't know what she meant.

Or why she was so damn suspicious of their guest?

Bishop stepped out of the barn then and stared after the pickup as Aubrey drove away. And there was some odd expression on his face, one almost of longing.

And Jasper had to acknowledge that maybe his sister was right not to trust this guy. Maybe there was something off about him, something not quite what it seemed…

But what?

What could Luke Bishop possibly be hiding?

Chapter 3

What was Luke Bishop hiding?

Using the computer at the reception desk in the main lodge, Aubrey scrolled through the guest's records. He'd paid with cash. No credit card on file, even for extra charges. Not that there had been any of those...

He'd eaten no meals in the main lodge. And he hadn't even made any phone calls on the landline in his cabin. Of course he probably had a cell phone, but the reception was so spotty out at the ranch that most guests used the landline.

Hell, he hadn't even rented a movie. What was he doing at his solitary cabin for entertainment, for companionship? He'd checked in alone.

That didn't mean that he hadn't met someone, though. But where?

He had to be going to town, buying his food or supplies there.

If she was going to give their guest the chance Jasper had asked her to give him, she needed to know more.

And she could think of only one way how…especially if he was dangerous, as she was now beginning to suspect.

Along with the guest records on file, there were also the codes for the automatic locks on every room and for every cabin. She made a mental note of his before grabbing the keys and heading back out to the pickup truck.

Not that she was going to search his place or invade his privacy…if he was there. And he probably was, since he'd been returning his horse to the barn instead of saddling up.

But if he was gone…

Maybe on one of those trips to town…

His cabin was the farthest from the main lodge and the barn. It was closer to the distant pastures, the ones where the cattle were that needed to be moved, closer to her house and to Jasper's. She loved sitting on her deck, staring at the snowy peaks in the distance as she sipped her coffee in the morning and an occasional glass of wine at night.

Alone…

Or so she'd thought, but Luke Bishop had been just a short walk away. Well, a short walk on the ranch; it was still a distance if they were in the city. If there had been other buildings and people between them…

But there were only pine trees and boulders and, out here where it was colder than in town, snow-covered grass.

And all her suspicions. She needed to know more about him and not just because she was entertaining the thought of his helping move the cattle but because he was so close.

Closer than she'd let anyone get in a while and not just physically. He was on her mind. And she didn't like it—and something about him worried her.

She didn't like that she'd been thinking of him ever since she'd gotten caught up in his gaze yesterday. That she'd wondered about that jolt of attraction she'd felt for him, had wondered if he'd felt it, too.

But he was probably married or involved with someone. Or worse yet, up to some kind of scam, like Warren had been.

She needed to know if he posed a threat to herself or anyone else on the property. So, instead of continuing down the road that led to Jasper's ranch house and then hers, she stopped at the cabin. There was no vehicle parked outside, so he must have gone into Blue Larkspur.

She could check out the cabin, but she hesitated, reluctant to invade a guest's privacy. But as a good hostess, she should make sure that he had everything he needed, that the cabin's small furnace was functioning properly, that none of the pipes were freezing. Or so she told herself.

She shut off the truck and pushed open the driver's door. Reciting the code to the lock beneath her breath, she walked up to the door. Before touching the buttons, she leaned close and listened.

But the wind picked up, whipping around the cabin.

The sound of it was all she heard, that and the howl of coyotes in the distance.

She quickly punched in the numbers. The lock clicked, and she pushed open the door and stepped out of the cold. The cabin wasn't much warmer inside or brighter. It was afternoon yet, but clouds blocked the sun, casting shadows everywhere—especially within the small log house.

Maybe Luke hadn't even returned here after going to the barn. He certainly hadn't turned on any lights or turned up the heat.

The place was tidy, so tidy that she wondered now if he'd checked out. If he'd left…

So much for his open-ended plans to stay.

But then her eyes adjusted to the dimness, and she noticed the boots at the door. Her pulse quickened with nerves. It was possible that he had more than one pair. Jasper certainly did, and her other brothers probably had as well.

But…

She hesitated about moving away from the door. And she cocked her head to listen, but even inside, all she heard was the wind, rushing around the cabin, hurtling against the windows. The storm was coming.

She needed to get to the cattle. It was too late to leave today. But tomorrow the livestock would have to be moved closer.

Just as she needed to move.

She stepped away from the door and noticed that other things, besides the boots, were inside the cabin. A laptop and some notebooks lay on the table next to the kitchenette. She opened one of the notebooks, but she couldn't read what was written inside. While the handwriting was bold and clear, the language was not. It definitely wasn't English.

But it looked beautiful, just like Luke Bishop's slight accent and his pale blue eyes.

Next to the laptop lay a battery, too small to have come from the computer but it had come from some electronic device. A phone?

She didn't see any...until she glanced into the trash bin next to the table. There were wadded up notes in there and not one but two disposable cells and the little chips that had come from them. The phones were broken, and those little chips looked mangled or burned.

"What the hell..." she murmured.

"Exactly," a deep voice said. "What the hell are you doing?"

She jumped and whirled around to the open door to the bedroom of the one-bedroom cabin. Luke stood, framed in the doorjamb, partially concealed in the shadows. For a moment, she thought he was naked, until she skimmed her gaze over his bare chest to where he'd knotted a towel at his lean waist. Her heart had been pounding fast and hard already, but now it pounded harder and faster.

"Damn..." she muttered.

Damn that she'd been caught snooping. But most of all, damn was he hot! So hot that heat rushed through her—the heat of attraction and the heat of embarrassment.

Luca fought to keep from grinning at her. He should have been furious that she'd let herself into the cabin, but the look on her face, the way she kept staring at him had male pride rushing through him, along with a hot wave of desire. He wanted to reach for her, wanted to pull her into his arms against his naked chest, wanted to lower his head to hers, brush his mouth across...

He cleared his throat of the desire choking him and repeated his question, albeit without the expletive. "What are you doing?"

When he stepped out of the shower, he'd realized that he was no longer alone—even though he'd been able to hear nothing but the wind.

There'd been a shift in the air, an awareness, an electricity.

At first he'd thought it was danger, but then he'd glanced out the window and noticed the truck parked out front. The Gemini Ranch truck...

And even though it could have been her brother who'd driven it here, he'd known it was her—because of that heightened energy in the cabin, in him.

But that didn't mean he wasn't in peril. Because he had a feeling that he was in uncharted territory with Aubrey Colton.

"You offered to help move the cattle," she said.

He glanced around the small cabin. "I don't see any of them in here. Why did you let yourself inside?"

"The door wasn't locked," she said, but she didn't meet his gaze when she made the claim.

The lie...

He always made sure to lock doors and windows and to double-check that they were secure, to make sure nobody could sneak in while he was sleeping. Not that he slept all that much or that soundly.

"So you just let yourself inside?" he asked.

"It's going to get cold tonight—"

"So you're here to keep me warm?" he interrupted to tease her.

Her face flushed, and she met his gaze now, her eyes narrowed in a glare. "No. I came to check the furnace."

"But the furnace isn't on the table or in the trash can," he pointed out.

She'd found the broken burner phones. She had to be curious about those, about his notes, but hopefully she wasn't able to read Italian.

She gestured toward the door next to the kitchen cabinets. "It's in that closet. I was just about to check on—"

"—when I caught you looking in my trash can," he finished for her. "But you first said that you came here about my offer to help move the cattle."

Her head bobbed in a quick nod that had her golden blond hair bouncing around her shoulders. "Yes, that's why I'm here." A few pieces of her long bangs fell across her glasses. Instead of pushing them away, she blew out a breath that chased them back into place.

He wished he'd been close enough to feel that breath, to taste it, so he stepped out of the bedroom doorway and moved closer to her. The cabin was small. In two strides, he was standing right in front of her, right in front of his laptop. Even if she'd opened it, it was protected with a special, encrypted password and facial identification. She wouldn't have been able to access anything on it. His book.

His life…

"Moving the cattle or checking the furnace?" he asked with the same abruptness he used when interviewing reluctant subjects or witnesses. "Which is your real reason for breaking into my cabin?"

"I—I didn't break in," she said even as her face flushed, and her gaze dropped from his eyes to his chest.

"Or do you have some other reason for seeking me out, Ms. Colton?" he asked less abruptly, but he still wanted an answer.

She took a step back so quickly that she nearly stumbled. He reached out and caught her shoulders, steadying her. But she quickly tugged away from him. "I came here to talk to you about the cattle and then it occurred to me that I should check the furnace."

"So you just let yourself in?"

"I didn't think you were home." She gestured toward the window. "There was no vehicle outside."

"I don't have one..." He'd taken the bus from Boulder to Blue Larkspur, paying cash for the bus ticket and the fare for the cab that had brought him out to the ranch from town.

"Why not?"

He shrugged. "Does it matter? Surely we're going to use horses to move the cattle?"

"Sometimes we use trucks," she said. Or they made sure trucks were close by, in case they needed medical assistance for hands or veterinarian services for the livestock. "But these pastures aren't accessible by vehicle."

"Which is one of the reasons I assume you need the cattle moved closer," he concluded.

She nodded. "The snow could make it too hard to get feed to them."

He glanced toward the window, where the sky had gone dark. "Do we need to leave now?"

"You're a little underdressed," she said and smiled. "Especially with the storm coming, you might get cold."

He should have been cold now; he hadn't turned up the furnace when he'd returned from his ride. But after his long walk from the barn, the cabin had felt much warmer than it had been outside. And now with the way she kept looking at him, his blood was pumping hot and fast through him—heating him up from the inside out. He couldn't resist teasing her some more and said, "You won't keep me warm?"

"You would have better luck with the cattle," she told him, and even though her lips were still curved into that smile, her voice was serious as she clearly offered him the warning that he wasn't going to get close to her.

"So I better get dressed, then," he said.

She nodded and released a quiet breath. But then she added, "We won't ride out until tomorrow morning, though. We'll have time before the storm hits to move them."

He nodded now. "If that's the case, you could have called and let me know." On the wall next to the cabinets of the kitchenette hung a landline telephone with a direct connection to the main lodge.

"I pass this cabin on my way home," she said.

"The big house at the end of the road—that's yours?" he asked, his pulse quickening at the thought of how close he was to her and she was to him…

Maybe too close, if he was found again.

But he couldn't be found again. He had to be safe somewhere, and for some reason, he hoped that Gemini Ranch was that somewhere.

She nodded. "Yes. That's mine." And there was pride

and satisfaction in her voice. This was a woman who worked hard and took care of herself—a strong, independent woman.

But she could still be hurt. Just like his family and friends back in Naples.

"This is dangerous, you know," she murmured.

And he wondered if she was talking about the cattle or about this attraction that sizzled between them. She had to feel it, too, he could tell from the way she kept looking at him.

"I have worked as a ranch hand before," he assured her. "I know what I'm doing."

"What do you do now?" she asked, and she looked away from him to the laptop.

"I—I…" Didn't want to lie to her. But he didn't want her in danger, either, and anyone who knew the truth about him, who knew his true identity, could be in danger. "I'm writing a book. Or at least I'm trying…"

"Writer's block?" she asked.

"I am struggling," he admitted. With as often as he'd had to move to stay ahead of the Camorra, he hadn't been able to focus on his writing. Only on the danger.

"Is that why you smashed the phones?" she asked. "Editor or agent bothering you for the finished product?"

"Something like that."

"My brother Gavin is a writer," she said. "Well, maybe he's more of a journalist. He has a podcast called *Crime Time*."

A gasp slipped between Luca's lips.

"You know him?" she asked, and now she beamed with pride in her sibling.

Luca nodded even as his stomach knotted with apprehension. Gavin had reached out to interview him before Luca had learned about that hit taken out on him. "I've streamed an episode or two. I thought he was based out of New York City or Chicago." And he hoped like hell he was still there and not here, where he might recognize Luca.

"He lives in New York, but he was born and raised in Blue Larkspur just like the rest of us," she said with a smile of affection for her family.

"How many of you are there?" he wondered.

Her smile widened. "Twelve."

And Luca inhaled sharply. "Your parents were very busy."

Her smile slipped away. "Well, there were several multiple births like me and Jasper."

"You're twins?"

She nodded. "Gemini…"

"Oh, of course…" That explained the origin of the name of the ranch.

"We're the second set," she said. "My oldest siblings, Caleb and Morgan, were the first set. Followed by triplets, Oliver, Ezra and Dominic…"

"Wow," he murmured. "Your poor mother,"

"You have no idea," she said, and there was something in her voice, something poignant about her tone.

"After the triplets, there were two single births, Rachel and Gideon, then Jasper and I came along, and next was Gavin. Maybe that's why he's such a loner."

Luca could relate: he was an only child. But his extended family was big with many aunts and uncles and cousins. He'd been closest to Paolo. Maybe too close…

for Paolo's safety. Unlike Luca's mother and aunt, his cousin had refused to go into hiding. He believed he was safe, even after all the murders the Camorra had committed to intimidate and punish.

"But Gavin wasn't the youngest for very long before the last set of twins were born," she continued. "Alexa and Naomi." She heaved a heavy sigh, as if reciting her family tree had exhausted her.

The affection on her beautiful face and in her voice when she spoke of her big family took his breath away. Family was important to her. He understood because he would do anything—even stay away—to keep his family safe.

"Will any of your siblings be helping us move the cattle?" he asked.

"Jasper, of course," she said. "And hopefully we'll be able to recruit some of the others, if they're not too busy." She pointed at his laptop. "Are you sure you're not too busy? Don't you have a deadline you need to meet?"

His shoulders stooped slightly. "Yes."

"If you're struggling, I can see if Gavin could talk to you, offer some pointers. I know journalism is probably quite different from writing a book, unless…" She narrowed her eyes behind her lenses and studied him. "Are you writing about something true?"

Too true.

He shook his head. "No. Fiction. Entirely made-up." *I wish.* And he wished even more that he didn't have to lie to her. But just in case she'd recognized any of the words in his notes, it was better that she thought anything about the Camorra was just from his imagination and not the frightening reality of the murderous gangs.

"Then I don't know if Gavin can help…"

"I appreciate the offer," he assured her—though he had no intention of speaking to her brother and was glad he was far away from Blue Larkspur. Since Gavin Colton had heard enough about him to reach out for an interview, he probably would have been able to recognize him.

At thirty-eight, Luca had been a journalist for a long time, nearly a decade longer than Gavin Colton, but he wasn't often recognized outside Europe, despite all the high-profile exposés he'd done. The Camorra had been just one of many, but they were certainly the most dangerous—since they'd put out the official hit on him.

"And I appreciate you offering to help with the cattle," she said. "But not if it's going to be any trouble to you…"

The deadline wasn't the problem. Yet. But Aubrey Colton might be.

Even if the Camorra didn't find him.

"I think the fresh air helps clear my head," he said. "That is why I go riding so often." And because he felt so restless, so on edge…

Would he ever be safe anywhere?

Would he ever get his life back?

Or would the Camorra keep coming for him until his life was over?

"You will get plenty of fresh air tomorrow," she said, as she turned and headed toward the door. "But I suggest that you dress a little warmer…" Her gaze slid over his chest again and down further…

His body began to tighten, to react…

He could almost imagine that she was touching him, her hands sliding over his bare skin…

His breath caught in his throat, nearly choking him.

And she chuckled, a sexy little chuckle. She knew that she was getting to him. "I will be sticking close to you tomorrow," she said, her voice just above a husky whisper. "Really close…"

His chest moved with the force of his pounding heart. "I thought you weren't going to keep me warm?" he reminded her of her warning.

"I'm not," she said. "I just want to keep you alive…" Then she opened the door and stepped out.

So she missed what Luca murmured in response. She missed him saying, "I wish you could…"

Paolo's phone vibrated against his desk again, and he hastened to answer it. He knew it wasn't going to be Luca. His calls were never this close together. So it had to be…

"You better be right this time," the caller warned him before even making certain it was him.

"I am," Paolo said. "A dude ranch in Blue Larkspur. The tracker I had on my phone revealed his location in Colorado, and that's the only ranch that takes guests through the winter. Luca has to be at the Gemini Ranch."

"So are the assassins," he was assured. "As long as this is really where Rossi is, he will be eliminated."

"He was at all the other places," Paolo said in his own defense. "He's just smart, observant. He caught on to the 'accidents' that were supposed to befall him."

"These assassins will eliminate Rossi by whatever means necessary, and they don't care about collateral damage. This has gone on long enough—the man has lived too long with his betrayal. He is beginning to make even more of a mockery of us. He has to die. Soon, or…"

Paolo would die. He'd been given that ultimatum a while ago; he knew the expiration date was running out on it. He'd already been in deep to the Camorra, for the money they'd loaned him for his car dealership, for the exorbitant interest that compiled on that "loan" and for the other debts he'd compiled for their "help" in eliminating his competition.

The Camorra was calling in his debts now, and he had to pay up with his cousin's life.

If Luca wasn't dead soon, Paolo would be. So Luca had to die…

Chapter 4

I wish you could...

Just as Aubrey was pulling the cabin door shut, she heard what Luke Bishop had whispered. *I wish you could...*

She probably should have stepped back inside and asked why he'd said that, what he meant, but she didn't expect him to answer her truthfully. So she walked out to her truck and, her hand shaking a bit in reaction to their encounter, jammed the key in the ignition and started it. Then she drove the too-short distance down the road to her house.

After parking, she pushed open her door and hurried toward her house. It was a hybrid between a log home and an A-frame, with tall windows that looked over the front deck and the property. Thanks to the glass French doors, it was always bathed in light. But for now...

Now the sky was growing dark, casting long shadows into her home. She unlocked the doors and stepped inside, but instead of starting a fire, she reached instead for her phone.

She needed to call in those reinforcements, and not just for moving the cattle…

As her hand closed around it, her phone vibrated with an incoming text. Maybe Jasper had already called their siblings with requests for help. But he would have asked just for assistance with the cattle, not with what she wanted done…

She needed help getting some information.

She swiped her cell screen to read the text and found that it wasn't from a Colton at all.

Please, Aubrey, give me a chance to prove to you how much I care…

She snorted in derision at Warren's message. The only thing he cared about was himself and his gambling debts. His creditors must have been getting impatient for their money.

Aubrey was getting impatient as well. Maybe she should have blocked him, like Jasper had said. But getting these texts reminded Aubrey of how she'd nearly been duped. Of how she shouldn't trust her judgment when it came to men.

Not that Warren was much of a man, not when he wanted someone else to clean up the mess he'd made. He was more like a child in his personality—and especially in comparison to Luke Bishop.

Now, *there* was a man. Heat flushed Aubrey's entire

body when she thought of him. His chest bare but for a smattering of black hair on his lean body, washboard abs and the hip bones that had jutted over the top of that low-hanging towel.

That towel hadn't hidden much from her imagination. Yet, she suspected that Luke was hiding something. Why smash those phones and destroy the chips inside? Or was he in hiding?

Was that why he'd made that cryptic comment? Or had she just imagined that?

It had been windy outside; it howled around her house now. The heat of her desire for her guest faded away, leaving her chilled and oddly frightened.

She'd accepted his offer to help move the cattle, but that didn't mean she trusted him. In fact, she trusted him even less now than she had before. Everything she'd seen had only reinforced her uneasiness around him, that sense of danger she'd picked up on the very first time their gazes had locked.

Ignoring Warren's text as she had all of his other ones, she swiped through her contacts to the C's. And in the long list of Coltons, she chose Dominic.

He was an FBI agent—he would know if Luke Bishop was on a most-wanted list.

Standing in that small cabin, with him barely dressed, she'd wanted him. Too much. Wanted him still, even knowing that she shouldn't trust him. But maybe she didn't have to trust him as long as she knew not to let her heart get involved.

If she knew exactly what and whom she was dealing with…

"Hey, Aub," Dominic answered. "Jasper sent out the

text already. I'd love to help, but I can't get away from Denver right now."

"I don't need your help with the cattle," she said. Though she could have used it. "I have another favor to ask you."

"Shoot," he said, getting right to the point in his usual no-nonsense manner.

Aubrey smiled, imagining him running a hand through his shaggy dark blond hair as he waited for her request. "I want you to find out everything you can about one of our guests."

She waited for the why and wondered how she would explain this gut feeling she had. This…

"What's his name?" Dominic asked instead.

"Luke Bishop," she replied. But remembering that notebook filled with writing in some other language, she wondered. Bishop didn't sound very European, unlike Luke's subtle and sexy accent.

"Do you have a date of birth?" he asked. "Driver's license number? Social security?"

"No."

"What about his credit card?"

"No, he paid cash."

"Thought you had to have a credit card on file for additional room charges," Dominic said. "Or damages…"

"He made an additional cash deposit for incidentals and damages." But nothing had been credited to it. No meals. No calls…

"What do you know about this guy?" Dominic asked.

That he looked damn good in nothing but a towel. But she definitely wasn't going to admit that to her older brother. "He's probably late thirties. Claims to be a writer…"

"You don't think he is?"

"I don't know." She sighed. "But maybe he is." He'd certainly seemed to recognize Gavin's name.

"Are you interviewing the guy for a job?" Dominic asked. "Are you just looking for a background check on him?"

"If he'd filled out an application, we can do that ourselves," she said. Then she would have had his social security number and his date of birth. "I think he's probably mid-thirties." She remembered the gray at his temples and in his stubble; there had even been a few silver strands in the hair on his sculpted chest. "Maybe late thirties…"

"Anything else?"

She swallowed hard as she remembered and wondered…

"I found some things in his trash can. Some notes that weren't written in English and some broken up cell phones."

"Are you cleaning rooms now?" Dominic asked. "Or searching them? What's the deal with this guy, Aub? What's made you so suspicious of him?"

There it was: the why.

And she wasn't sure she could honestly answer. She wasn't sure what it was about Luke Bishop that just didn't feel right.

Or maybe it was that he felt too right, too handsome, too charming, too intriguing…

"I don't know," she admitted. "I just have this feeling…" Too much feeling for a stranger—a very strange stranger at that. Maybe that was what fascinated her so much about him, that he seemed unlike anyone else she'd ever met. And she'd met a lot of people over the years that she and Jasper had been running their business.

Aubrey held her breath as she waited, wondering if her vague answer would be good enough for Dominic to check out her mysterious guest.

"You didn't give me a whole hell of a lot to go on," he told her. "But I'll see if I can find out anything."

"Thank you," she said.

"Just…" Dominic began, "since you have this feeling, keep your distance from Luke Bishop until I can check him out."

She couldn't promise that, not when she intended to do exactly the opposite. "Don't worry," she told him instead.

"I do," he said, "especially after that loser you dated last…"

She flinched just as her phone dinged with another text.

Warren: Please…

He could beg all he wanted, but she was never letting him get close to her again.

Now Luke Bishop.

She wanted to be close to him, curled up in his strong arms, tight against his bare chest, but she couldn't. Not when she didn't trust him.

I wish you could…

Maybe she'd just imagined that; maybe he hadn't said anything like that. Or maybe that feeling she had was right, and Luke Bishop was trouble. Hopefully, Dominic would be able to find out more about her enigmatic guest.

And in the meantime, she would stick close enough to Luke that he might reveal some of his secrets—because she had no doubt that the man had some.

But what kind of secrets? Secrets like her father had kept from his family?

The walk to the barn the morning after Luca had found Aubrey Colton in his cabin was a long one. The temperature had definitely dropped, and the wind was fierce, but only a few flurries swirled around the ground. The storm wasn't here yet, but it was coming.

Luca felt it, and he shivered more in anticipation than from the cold. He could have gotten a ride from Aubrey; she'd driven past his cabin. But whenever he heard a vehicle, his first instinct was to slip out of sight, to watch and wait and hope like hell that it wasn't someone coming for him.

So when he'd heard the rumble of her pickup, he'd slipped into the pines around his cabin and waited. He could have come out when Aubrey had stopped. But then he would have had to explain…

No, he would have had to lie to her again, and he hadn't wanted to do that. So he'd waited while she stalled for several long moments before driving off again.

She hadn't gone up to the door. She hadn't knocked. Or let herself in as she had the day before. She hadn't even tooted her horn. Maybe she was hoping he'd changed his mind about helping.

Or maybe she just hadn't wanted to catch him as she had yesterday. Half-naked...

He'd barely been able to sleep for thinking about how she'd looked at him. How flushed she'd been, despite the chilly air in the cabin.

She had to feel this, too—this attraction between them. But it couldn't go anywhere, couldn't lead to anything but danger for her and heartache for him.

Luca couldn't act on that attraction. But he could help her with the cattle. Surely, nobody had found him yet. The only people he'd encountered since coming to Gemini Ranch were the receptionist at the check-in desk, Jasper, Aubrey and a few of the ranch hands.

Kayla was the one he found first in the barn when he stepped inside it. She was saddling a horse, her arms rippling with her lean muscles. Like Aubrey, she was a strong woman.

"Are you going with us?" he asked.

She shook her head, and her dark brown ponytail swished across her back. "No, I'm needed here," she remarked with a trace of resentment. "New guests arrived yesterday and have signed up for riding lessons at the indoor ring."

"You don't like giving lessons?" he asked. As a journalist his first instinct was always to question everything and everyone—often to his family's annoyance. A pang of longing over missing them struck his heart.

She shrugged. "It's fine. I just prefer ranching."

"What about your bosses?" he asked.

"What about them? They probably make more money off having guests than they do off the livestock and the land."

"I meant, how are they as bosses?" he wondered. Especially about Aubrey...

"They're great," she said but without a whole lot of enthusiasm. Then, almost as if speaking to herself, she added beneath her breath, "Their dad ruined my life, but they're great."

"What?" he asked, shocked.

She sighed and shook her head. "I'm sorry. I shouldn't have said that. You're a guest—"

"I'm helping out with moving the cattle today," he said. "I'd like to know more about the people I'm working for."

"You're not working for their dad," she said. "He's been dead for twenty years."

And Kayla couldn't be a whole lot older than twenty—maybe five or six years—so how had their father ruined her life?

"I'd like to know more," he told her. He would like to know everything about Aubrey Colton, like how her skin felt, how her lips tasted...

Another pang struck him—this one of lust. He closed his eyes for a moment and willed it away before focusing on Kayla again.

"What did her—*their*—father do?" he prodded the female ranch hand.

But she just shook her head again. "I'm not dredging all that up again. It's too late now anyways."

He wasn't sure what she meant by that. If it was too late because what had happened had already happened, or if there just wasn't enough time for her to tell him about it without anyone else overhearing them. Because he heard other voices now, and he turned to see

Aubrey walking toward him from another area of the mammoth barn.

She wasn't alone. A tall man with medium brown hair walked beside her, so close that their shoulders bumped. And something churned inside Luca, twisting his stomach with dread and...

Jealousy?

Was that what this nauseous feeling was? He'd never experienced it before. Had never gotten attached enough to anyone to ever feel possessive of them...

Not that he was attached to Aubrey Colton. He barely knew her. But what he knew intrigued him. She was strong and smart and so incredibly sexy with her curvy body.

And something about the way she looked at him, through the lenses of those black-framed glasses, stirred something deep and almost primal inside him. He wanted her. Too much...

And when she turned her head and laughed at something the man said, he sucked in a breath at what felt like a blow to his stomach.

Or maybe to his pride.

He'd thought she'd been interested in him. Attracted to him.

But he must have just imagined it all. Because clearly, she had a close relationship with whoever this guy was. And for some reason that made Luca hate him before he even met the guy.

So this was the guy?

The one that had Aubrey all unsettled and edgy? Since Gideon had showed up that morning, his younger sister had been acting odd. Distracted. Moody.

Gideon studied the older man with curiosity and some amusement. The guy stared back at him, his pale blue eyes icy cold. As a social worker, Gideon had dealt with a lot of animosity. Parents were rarely happy to see him—unless he was reuniting a family. Unfortunately, he wasn't able to do that as often as he would like. But the children were always his first priority.

Children. Then family…

He'd hoped by now to have one of his own. But at least he had his siblings and his mom. He'd thought once that he'd had someone else—*the* someone else—that special person with whom he could start that family he wanted.

"Gideon," Aubrey said.

And he realized he was the one who was distracted now. "Yes?"

"This is Luke Bishop," Aubrey introduced him to the tall stranger. "And, Luke, this is my brother Gideon."

The stranger's eyes immediately warmed, and he offered Gideon a grin along with his hand. Gideon shook it, marveling at the strength and the calluses. Maybe the guy would be able to handle himself with the ranch work.

But what about Aubrey?

She was tough. But not nearly as tough as she thought she was. Despite what she'd claimed, that idiot Warren Parker had dealt quite a blow to her ego—if not her heart.

"So she roped you into helping move the cattle," Luke remarked, his voice deep with a curious accent. Gideon wondered where he was from but refrained from asking.

"He just stopped by to visit the horses, like he often does, and I enlisted him. I am very good at roping," Aubrey said with pride.

Gideon nodded. "She is. She and Jasper played cowgirl and cowboy all the time growing up. And they lassoed everything in the house—the newel post on the stairwell, the trash can, the family dog and even the rest of us if we didn't move fast enough."

Aubrey nudged his shoulder with hers. "*You* never moved fast enough."

He chuckled.

So did Luke. "So you didn't move fast enough this time, either."

"No, but I actually enjoy coming out to the ranch," Gideon admitted. Any time spent doing the physical labor in the fresh air was a welcome respite from the emotional demands of his job. "It's not often she ropes a guest into working, though, unless they've signed up for the cattle drives."

"I offered," Luke admitted. "But I think she's going to charge me extra for this *experience*."

"That depends on how much extra work you make this," Aubrey said. She glanced at her watch. "You're already late. We need to get saddled up and get going."

Luke touched his fingers to the brim of his hat in a mocking salute. "Yes, boss. I'll be ready in just a few moments." With a grin he headed past them to one of the stalls, like he already had a horse here and he knew where everything was.

For a guest, he seemed awfully comfortable at the ranch and with Aubrey. Gideon studied him for a moment before turning to study his sister.

"So where do you want me, *boss*?" Gideon asked her. "With you or with Luke?"

"You're riding with Jasper. Luke's riding with me," she said, almost possessively.

"What's going on with you two?" he asked with some curiosity.

Aubrey was usually very adamant that guests were off-limits for dating—for her and Jasper and for their siblings. Their brother Oliver was the only one she'd really needed to be concerned about, though. He'd always been a heartbreaker.

She shook her head. "Nothing. He's a guest."

"A guest who seems really comfortable with you," Gideon remarked.

She shrugged. "That's just his personality."

She didn't seem too upset about it, but Gideon wondered if that was why she was so edgy. The guy was getting to her. "Is that all it is? Is he something more to you than a guest?"

"No, absolutely not," she replied a little too vehemently.

"That's too bad," Gideon said. "You deserve to have someone special in your life." Especially after how Warren Parker had tried to use her.

"I don't have time," she said. "Not with the ranch and now the new case that the Truth Foundation has taken on." She uttered a ragged sigh. "I feel bad that I don't help out more with the foundation."

He reached out and squeezed her shoulder. "You carry a lot of responsibility already. Don't worry about it. Focus on yourself and…" He grinned and glanced over at the stall Luke had slipped into. "…maybe on finding that certain someone…"

She smiled at him. "You're the one who deserves someone special."

He'd had someone like that. Once. But he'd come on too strong and lost her. He forced a smile. "I'm fine."

At least he was better than Aubrey seemed at the moment. She kept glancing toward that stall where Luke had gone. In anticipation or trepidation?

He was usually pretty empathetic and could pick up on the emotions of others, which served him well when kids were so often reluctant to share their feelings. Or afraid to…

Was that Aubrey's problem? Was she afraid to fall again? Afraid to risk her heart, only to have it broken?

Or was there another reason she was afraid of Luke Bishop?

Chapter 5

He was good. Really good…

As comfortable as he seemed to be in the saddle, he was equally comfortable with the cattle—directing them through the open gates in the fence from one pasture to the next.

But Aubrey wasn't convinced yet that he hadn't told her other lies. Like Warren had…

Like their father had told their mother and them. So many.

Wondering how truthful Luke Bishop had been with her, Aubrey glanced over at him now as they rode side by side back to the barn from the pastures that were close to the riding ring. They'd moved a lot of livestock today but not all of them.

And while the wind continued to blow, the snow wasn't falling hard yet. Just big, soft flakes that floated down on them, sticking to their hats and onto their coats.

"Are you sure you don't want to return for the rest of them?" Luke asked even as he huddled in his jacket and turned his face from the wind that had already chafed his skin.

His work ethic impressed her, too. He'd been tireless the entire day, not even stopping for the lunch she'd brought, even eating his sandwich in the saddle.

He was nothing like the many guests who'd dropped out of the cattle drives over the years because it hadn't been as glamorous as they'd thought it was going to be. Who'd been surprised that it had actually been work.

Luke had already done more than she'd expected of him, so she shook her head. "No. We'll go back out early tomorrow morning. We'll have time before it gets bad. The worst of the storm isn't coming for a day or so. And hopefully, it's not going to be as bad as they're predicting." But if it was, they needed to be prepared.

Luke nodded. "You're the boss."

"One of them," she said. "Jasper and I are equal partners."

"You started this together?" he asked.

She nodded. "Yes. It was our dream since we were little kids."

"When you played cowgirl and cowboy all the time," he said.

She smiled at the memory Gideon had shared that morning. They were drawing closer to the barn, so she looked for Gideon's vehicle, but it was gone. He and Jasper must have returned already. Or Gideon had been called out on a case. Her smile slipped away at the thought. She didn't know how her older brother handled his heartbreaking job, especially given how empathetic he was.

She was glad she and her twin had chosen another path. "Yes," she replied to Luke. "Jasper and I always had our plan. What about you?"

"Did I play cowboy and cowgirl?" he asked. "I don't have a sister or a brother."

She sucked in a breath at the thought of not having her siblings. "That must have been very lonely for you."

He shook his head. "I have many cousins that lived close by, so I was never alone unless I wanted to be."

"Is that why you're here now?" she asked. "Because you want to be alone to write your book? Was it your plan to always be an author?"

"So many questions," he said, his body suddenly tense in the saddle.

Clearly her questions unsettled him. But he'd shared some information about his life, so she'd thought he was willing to open up. She persisted. "Do you have a problem with questions?"

He murmured, almost beneath his breath. "No. Just that I'm usually the one asking them…"

"What?" she asked, uncertain if she'd heard him correctly, like the other night.

"I—I just prefer to ask the questions," he admitted. "I was a curious kid, probably why I'm a writer."

"Seems like that inquisitive nature would have led you to be a reporter," she remarked, "since you like asking questions."

He swung out of the saddle—on the side away from her, as if he suddenly wanted to hide, as if he'd revealed too much.

But she hadn't even asked all the questions she had for him. "Where did you grow up?" she asked. "I can't quite place your accent…"

"What accent?" he asked, and he grinned at her over the back of her horse.

"Exactly," she said. "What kind of accent is it?"

"The kind that usually makes the ladies swoon," he said, his smile widening as he flirted with her.

Aubrey swung down from the saddle, too, and led her horse through the barn doors Luke held open for her. "I'm not the swooning type." If she had been, she would have swooned last night when she'd seen him in nothing but that towel. She and Luke took off the bridles and hitched their mounts to crossties.

"I know," he said, watching as she removed the saddle from her horse and hefted it onto her shoulder. "Fortunately I prefer strong women."

She appreciated that he didn't try to help her as she carried the saddle to the tack room. He'd removed and carried his, their shoulders nearly brushing as he walked close beside her.

She'd strolled that way with Gideon that morning, but being next to Luke was entirely different. She felt tense and edgy and totally aware of him, of every brush of the sleeve of his jacket against her clothing. To take her mind off his proximity, she murmured, "I learned how to be strong from my mother."

Isadora Colton was the strongest woman Aubrey knew; she'd survived so much loss and humiliation. "She raised twelve kids, most of them on her own after my father died."

"I'm sorry," he said. "I heard that he passed away twenty years ago. You must have been young."

She tensed now. "What did you hear about him?" Despite how long he'd been gone, people had yet to forget or forgive everything he'd done—herself included. She couldn't forgive him for how he'd hurt and humiliated her mother, for how he'd lied to them and for how many other people he'd unjustly sentenced as a judge.

He shrugged. "Someone just mentioned in passing that he was dead."

"Yes, he died in a car accident."

"I'm sorry," he repeated. "That must have been difficult."

"It might have been more difficult if he had lived," she murmured.

"What?" he asked, obviously shocked—his blue eyes wide as he stared down at her.

"It's just…" she sighed "…he had some major legal issues. There was going to be a trial…" She shook her head. "I'd rather not dredge it all up again."

"I've heard that recently, too," he remarked.

"Is that why you don't answer questions?" she wondered. "You don't want to dredge up painful subjects?"

"I definitely don't want to cause pain," he said, and while his choice of words was odd, it was clear he was sincere.

"Your pain or someone else's?" she asked.

"Neither," he said, but then he emitted a soft sigh and added, "Unfortunately that's not always possible."

"Why not?" she asked. "Why can't we all just be open and honest? That would save everyone a lot of heartache."

"Or cause even more," he said. "Sometimes the truth hurts."

Finding out the truth about her father certainly had, so Aubrey couldn't argue with him. But if only the Honorable Ben Colton hadn't done the things he had in the first place, then there would have been nothing to hide, no dishonor or disgrace...

No pain for any of the people his dishonesty had affected.

Tears stung her eyes, but she blinked them away. She was strong—too strong to dwell in the past over things she couldn't change. That was why her family had started the Truth Foundation—to change the things that they could.

And while Aubrey knew she couldn't change others' decisions, she could change herself. She could make sure she never fell for anyone she didn't fully trust.

And she certainly didn't trust Luke.

Not at all. Even though she was so incredibly attracted to him. That was why moments later, when she stopped outside his cabin, she shook her head when he asked if she wanted to come inside with him.

Just being this close to him—in the small cab of the pickup truck—had her skin hot and tingling with awareness, with attraction...

"No," she said. "That wouldn't be a good idea."

He didn't argue with her—didn't try to convince her. He just nodded in agreement. "You're right."

But why was she right? Because he was a guest who was just passing through, or was there another reason?

Like he was married?

Or a criminal?

Either way, Luke Bishop was a risk Aubrey wasn't willing to take. So she held her breath until he stepped out of the truck cab and closed the door.

Then she released it in a ragged sigh. And she tried to release the temptation to follow him as well. She was entirely too eager to do that.

Luke Bishop wasn't just physically attractive; he was intriguing as well. She wanted to know more about him, but she had a feeling that no matter how much she tried, she was never going to get out of him any answers for her questions. At least not any answers she could trust...

Stepping out of her truck, shutting the door and walking away from Aubrey Colton had been hard for Luca. He'd had such an enjoyable day with her, working beside her. Seeing how strong and capable she was had attracted him to her even more.

Maybe that was why he'd issued that ridiculous invitation for her to come inside with him. He hadn't wanted the day to end; he'd wanted to spend more time with her, talk to her more, look at her longer...

With no makeup, and her skin chafed from the cold, she was incredibly beautiful, natural and vibrant, and that was so damn sexy to him.

So it was good that she'd turned down his offer, that she'd remained in the truck while he walked to his cabin. She didn't stay in the driveway, though; she backed out and peeled away as if anxious to escape him. Hopefully, he hadn't made her uncomfortable—because even though he knew he couldn't offer her a future or even the present, he wanted to spend more time with her.

Working with her.

Talking with her.

But if he was found again, that would only put her in danger. No. It was better that she'd left. So Luca shook off his disappointment and proceeded to the door.

He wasn't sure why he checked, but before touching the buttons on the electronic lock, he tried the door and found it opened easily. It was not locked now. But he knew he'd locked it that morning, just as he had every time he left the cabin. Just like he had when he'd come out of his shower to find Aubrey inside, looking in his trash.

He'd spent the entire day with her, so she couldn't have been the one to unlock it. And he'd declined maid service when he'd checked in a little over a week ago, so nobody had come in to clean the place.

So who had been inside? Or was the person still there—waiting for him?

If only he had a gun or something he could use as a weapon…

Luca had always used his mind and his words to fight his battles in the past and to protect himself and those he cared about, but he doubted the Camorra had sent someone with whom he could reason his way out of danger.

Not danger. Murder. If the Camorra had sent someone for him, that person had come with Luca's death warrant. He glanced back toward the road, but Aubrey and her truck were gone.

That was good, though; he didn't want her in peril. But was she?

Was *he*?

The person he'd found in his cabin yesterday had been her, and while she'd been with him today, many staff members and her siblings lived in the area as well. Gideon and Jasper had returned before they had, leaving them time to search his cabin before he got back. Aubrey obviously had issues with trust. Because of her father? He resolved to research Aubrey's dad later, when he had time.

Whatever had happened hadn't ruined Aubrey's life; she'd achieved the dream she and her twin had had when they were children. But it might have been the reason she was so distrustful.

Or had another man broken her trust as well?

Or maybe she was just so smart that she knew Luca was hiding something and that he was lying about who he was.

Luca would rather believe that she was the one who had had his place searched. Then that meant that whoever had searched it posed no threat to him, or at least not the same threat the Camorra did. Because Luca was beginning to believe Aubrey posed a threat of another kind.

The kind he'd never encountered before, the kind where he might get attached…where he might fall for her. And that would only wind up hurting when he had to leave.

And he would have to leave…

Even if the Camorra hadn't found him yet, they might if he stayed in one place for too long. If he didn't keep moving around…

He needed to move now. Before pushing open the door, to see if anyone was still there, he looked around the immediate area. The tire tracks from her truck were the only ones in the fluffy, light snow. Luca inspected the steps, but there were no discernible prints from whoever had unlocked the door.

Whoever had gotten inside his place had likely done so a while ago; more than likely they had given up waiting for him and were already gone.

He raised his hand to the door again and pushed it open the rest of the way. The only way he would know was to go inside and check. He drew in a deep breath, just in case he was wrong…in case his intruder had stayed. But when he stepped inside, the cabin was cold and quiet and empty but for his belongings, which had been strewn around the small space. Fortunately, he'd hidden the things she'd found the other day—his laptop, the notebooks, the phones. But someone must have been searching for them, or perhaps for something else.

The doors of the kitchen cabinets had been left open, the drawers overturned. And through the doorway to the bedroom, he could see his clothes strewn around. What had they been looking for?

He stared at the phone, willing it to ring or vibrate with a text…to do anything but remain so damn stubbornly silent.

The assassins were there—more than one—at that dude ranch in Colorado. Surely, Luca wouldn't be able to escape this time. He wasn't that lucky, and he couldn't be as smart as he thought he was, either.

Or he would have figured it out by now…

He would have realized Paolo was betraying him, was helping the Camorra find him.

But he had no choice.

Would Luca realize that as well if he figured it out before he died? Would Luca understand that Paolo couldn't give up his life, even for Luca's?

Paolo had a wife. Well, an ex-wife now...

But he had kids. They were teenagers, and he barely saw them since they lived with their mother. But he had family. He had people who cared about him.

He had Luca.

Except for his mother, Luca had no immediate family of his own; his dad had died when he was just a child. So all he had was his career. His damn career that had caused so many problems, so many arrests and convictions...

And now—soon—it would cause Luca's own death...

Chapter 6

Aubrey had had to speed away from Luke's cabin so she wasn't tempted any more than she already was to stay with him. Or to turn around and go back to him.

When she'd left, the truck tires had spun on the snow-covered road. There wasn't much accumulation yet, just that light dusting—just enough to make the asphalt slick.

So she had to slow down for the rest of the trip to her house. But when she pulled into her driveway, she found another vehicle already parked there, and she wished she'd driven even slower.

Or better yet, that she'd stayed with Luke.

No. This—Warren Parker—was a good reminder of why she'd been smart not to stay with Luke Bishop. Warren was a good reminder that Aubrey shouldn't trust too early or too easily. Or maybe not at all...

Especially when someone avoided answering questions as much as Luke Bishop did. He had to be hiding something. But what?

Warren certainly wasn't hiding anything—because the minute she stepped out of her truck, he threw open the driver's door of his vehicle and ran up to her, reeking of desperation. His brown hair was disheveled, as if he'd been running his hands through it, and dark circles rimmed his brown eyes. "Aubrey, I've been texting you over and over, and you never reply. I've been so worried."

She didn't doubt that he'd been worried, but it hadn't been about her. "There's a reason I don't reply. I don't want to talk to you. So get back in your car and drive out of here."

He widened his eyes as if shocked at her words. "But we meant so much to each other…"

She laughed. "All I meant to you was a way to pay off your debts."

"I didn't take any money from you," he said.

"Because I refused to give you any," she reminded him. She was not a fool. Once he'd asked her to help him out, she'd figured out why he'd been so interested in her and had been so charming—because he'd wanted something from her. And then he'd been so angry that she hadn't fallen in with his plans that he'd actually admitted it.

"I'm not going to lie," he said—which probably indicated that he was. "It would have been nice if you'd given me a loan, if you could have helped me out. But that wasn't why I was with you, Aubrey. I only said that it was because I was upset. I felt rejected by you, and unlike other guys, I think you're beautiful."

"Unlike other guys..." she murmured. This was what he'd started doing with her, gaslighting her into thinking that if she wasn't with him, she would spend the rest of her life alone. Hell, she'd rather spend the rest of her life alone than with a creep like him. She definitely should have blocked his number.

"You know that other guys don't see what I see when I look at you," he said. "I find you attractive just the way you are." He smiled smugly—condescendingly—as if he was doing her a favor.

Her fingers curled into her palm, and she thought about throwing her gloved fist into his face. But from the fading yellow bruises around one of his eyes, it was clear someone else had beat her to beating up him. She shook her head, pitying him now. "You obviously owe someone a lot of money, Warren, but you're not going to manipulate me into giving it to you. So get the hell off my property."

He lurched forward then and gripped her arms. "Aubrey, you know we had something special. You know that you're important to me. Please, give me another chance. Nobody will ever treat you as well as I have. Nobody will ever give you the time and attention that I did."

She snorted. He'd always been busy with a game—playing poker—or watching a game, some sport on which he'd placed bets, that they'd actually spent very little time together over the months they'd dated.

How the hell had he thought she'd fallen for him so

hard that she'd pay off his debts? Did he really believe she was as desperate as he was?

That she was so undesirable she'd let him mess with her head and her self-esteem?

She nearly flinched as she felt a twinge of pain over some of the insults that had been hurled at her in the past. Kids had teased and picked on her in school. Her siblings had stepped in—had tried to protect her—but Aubrey had insisted that the petty remarks didn't bother her. And that she could take care of herself…

And she could and she had. Then and now. She knew better than to let anyone mess with her head or with her heart—like Warren was trying.

"Please, Aubrey," he implored her. "If you gave me another chance, we could have something real here—something lasting…"

She snorted again and shook her head. "Give it up, Warren. You're not fooling me again."

His hands tightened around her arms then, pinching her muscles, even through the thickness of her jacket. She could fight him off. While he was taller than she was, she was stronger—physically as well as mentally. She worked hard, whereas Warren only played hard and not too well.

But then she heard a sound behind her, bootheels crunching over the gravel drive as someone joined them. Had Warren been accompanied by someone else?

Or had someone followed him here?

She could get rid of her ex, but she wasn't sure she could fend off two people. And for the first time, real fear surged through Aubrey when she realized how alone and vulnerable she was.

Even if she screamed, Jasper's house was too far from hers for him to hear her. And Luke's cabin was nearly as far...

Not that Aubrey was looking for anyone to rescue her; she was no damsel in distress.

Anger coursed through Luca. He'd walked over to Aubrey's house to confront her over his searched cabin, but he'd quickened his pace as soon as he saw her in the distance with another man. He didn't like the way that man was holding Aubrey, his hands wrapped so tight around her arms. And his face was red—either from the cold or from struggling with her. Not that Aubrey appeared to be struggling much.

Was this man her boyfriend?

He certainly wasn't one of her brothers—not with the predatory way he was acting. Then the stranger suddenly released her and doubled over, gasping in pain.

Aubrey whirled around to him, her fists raised and ready to swing.

He held up his hands. "Don't hit me."

Though with the way the other man coughed and sputtered, Luca suspected she hadn't hit him with her fists but with her knee. Between gasps of pain, the man whined, "Aubrey, sweetheart, why did you do that..."

"Sweetheart..."

Who the hell was this simpering fool?

"You know why, Warren. Get in your car, get off my property and leave me the hell alone!"

"It was all a misunderstanding," the guy insisted. "You and I have too much going for us to give up so easily."

Clearly this person wasn't willing to give up easily, no matter how emphatically Aubrey told him she wanted nothing to do with him. Luca's heart lifted at the thought of that, and that sick feeling churning in his stomach when he'd seen her in the arms of another man was gone.

"Darling," Luca said to her. "Who is this man? And why is he bothering you?"

She arched a blond brow above the rim of her glasses. *"Darling?"*

"Yes," Luca said, infusing his tone with affection along with confusion. "Doesn't he realize that you're seeing me now, that you've moved on?"

Finally the man turned toward Luca, and his dark eyes widened as he stared him up and down. "You're—you're her boyfriend?" he asked, skepticism in his voice and in his beady eyes.

With all his traveling and riding, Luca knew he had lost some weight; he probably looked skinny, and with the silver creeping in at his temples and in his scruff, he probably appeared a whole lot older than Aubrey. But she hadn't looked at him last night, when he'd been wearing nothing but a towel, like she'd found him undesirable. While she might not feel the attraction for him that Luca felt for her, she hadn't been completely unaffected.

Was she still hung up on this guy—despite her rejection of his appeals for another chance?

That feeling was back, that sick jealousy swirling inside him. Luca closed the distance between himself and Aubrey. He slid his arm around her shoulders and pulled her against his side. "Yes, I am her boyfriend," he lied. "So do as the lady told you and get the hell off her property."

"Don't make me call security, Warren," she warned.

"That won't be necessary," Luca said, and he dropped his arm from her shoulders. He stepped closer to the other man, who still couldn't stand up straight after she'd kneed him in the groin. "I will get rid of him…"

Already injured, Warren must not have been spoiling for another fight, because he finally moved toward his car, his hand shaking as he reached for the door handle. But then he turned back to say, "Aubrey, you can't be serious about this guy. You and I haven't been broken up long enough for you to have gotten to know him well. Obviously he's just after your money."

"Like you were, Warren?" she asked. "Give it up. You're not getting a dime out of me. You're going to need to find another way to pay off your debts."

His jaw clenched as if he was grinding his teeth, but he didn't argue with her. He only glared at Luca before pulling open his door and sliding behind the wheel.

Not trusting Warren to not try to run him down, Luca reached out and tugged Aubrey with him toward the porch on the front of her house. Then he kept his arm wrapped around her while the guy drove off, feeling her body tremble slightly against his.

"Are you all right?" he asked with concern. "Did he hurt you?"

She snorted dismissively. "He's the one hurting right now."

But Luca wasn't so sure that she hadn't been harmed as well. "You're shaking."

"I'm just cold," she said. But instead of snuggling

into him—into his warmth—she pulled away and opened the door to her house.

When Luca had found that someone had searched his cabin again, he'd been so hot with anger toward her that he hadn't felt the cold on his fast walk from his place to hers. And when he'd seen how that man was holding her, his temperature had gone up even higher. So he didn't mind standing outside on the porch even with the wind picking up. "Who the hell is that man?"

"A mistake," she murmured. Even though she'd opened the door, she had yet to step inside what looked like a big, open room. Instead she turned back to look at him. "And a reminder to be very careful about who I trust…"

"Is that why you had someone search my place again?" he asked.

Above the rims of her glasses, her brow furrowed. "What are you talking about?"

"While we were out moving the cattle, someone broke into my cabin again. They must have been looking for something."

"Again?" she asked.

"Have you already forgotten that I caught you searching it yesterday?"

Her gaze slid away from his and she turned to step inside her house. In case she was going to shut him out, he stepped forward—making sure he got his foot in the door before she could close it on him. Not that he suspected that would stop her if she really wanted to get rid of him…

Remembering what she'd done to her ex-boyfriend, Luca braced himself for a blow or a well-placed knee.

But instead she opened the door wider and said, "Get inside. It's freezing."

The snowflakes were still fat and light, but they were starting to fall harder now. The storm that was forecast was intensifying, along with Luca's attraction to Aubrey Colton. He wasn't certain he should join her inside, just as she'd been reluctant to be alone with him in his cabin.

But if she really hadn't been the one who'd searched his place, he needed to know—because he needed to leave Gemini Ranch before anyone got hurt. So he followed her into her house. With its wood beams and rustic furnishings, it reflected her earthy, no-nonsense style.

She headed toward the stone hearth in the center of the great room and started a fire. Then she held out her hands to the flickering flames that reminded him of other blazes.

That B and B in Toronto…that hotel in Wisconsin.

Nobody had been hurt in either fire. But it could have been bad. Innocent people could have died because Camorra assassins had committed arsons to kill him.

"I shouldn't be here," he said as a sudden pressure settled on his chest, on his lungs, making it hard to breathe.

"You invited me to come into your cabin earlier," she reminded him.

"And you were smart to turn me down," he admitted.

She sighed. "I'm not always smart, or I never would have dated such a loser. You didn't have to act like that…"

He cocked his head. "Like what?" Like a jealous idiot?

"Like you're my boyfriend," she said. "He didn't believe it, anyway."

"Why not?" he asked. "Am I not your type?"

She tilted her head and studied him. "Unfortunately, you probably are…"

"Tall, dark and handsome?" he teased her.

"Not entirely open or honest," she corrected him.

And he flinched but he couldn't deny it.

"That's not what he meant, though," she said. "He's always been disparaging about my appearance."

Luca's jaw dropped. "What? That man is definitely a liar. How dare he insult you!" And now he wished he had hit Warren. Hard.

She shrugged, but it was as if a burden still remained on her shoulders. "He just tries to mess with my mind, tries to make me think that nobody else will want me but him. And he only wants my money—"

"Then he's an idiot as well as a liar," Luca said, his outrage boiling over. "How can he not see how beautiful you are? How amazing?"

Her eyes narrowed behind her lenses. "Aren't you laying it on a bit thick?"

He stepped forward then and tipped up her face to his. "You are so beautiful. Your eyes such a deep blue and so full of intelligence. Your body…" his mouth dried out just thinking about it, about her curves "…is strong and sexy…"

Her eyes widened with surprise, as her pupils dilated. She leaned forward a bit, as if waiting for him to kiss her. He wanted to, so badly, but when he began to lower his head toward hers, she pulled back and dislodged his hand from her chin. "You don't have to say this…"

"I don't have to," he agreed. "But it's true, and I hope you know it and that you would never let a creep like Warren affect your self-esteem."

She shook her head. "Of course not. I wouldn't…"

"But what?" he asked because he heard the *but* in her voice, the reluctance to let the man's awful comments go.

"When I was growing up, I got picked on sometimes," she admitted. "Girls can be cruel…" She shrugged again. "It's nothing. I didn't let it get to me then, and I certainly won't let Warren Parker get to me now."

"I'm so glad you kneed him," he said. "I wish you had done it so hard that he couldn't have walked, though."

"But then he wouldn't have been able to leave," she pointed out. And she clearly had wanted him gone as badly as Luca had.

"And he'd better stay away," Luca said.

Her lips curved into a slight smile. "You know you're not really my boyfriend, right? You don't have to act like you're jealous."

Luca released a shaky sigh. "The sad part is that I'm not acting…" And he couldn't remember the last time— if ever—that he'd felt jealousy like this.

The smile slid away from her mouth. "But you're not my boyfriend," she repeated. "Remember—I want someone that I can trust completely."

His heart ached that he couldn't be that man, but there was so much that he couldn't tell her, that he couldn't share with her, without putting her in danger. He glanced toward the door now, wondering if her life was in peril just because of him coming here to Gemini Ranch and now to her house.

What if whoever had been in his place had hung around and followed him here? But if the Camorra had sent someone, they wouldn't have been hired to just follow him. They would've been hired to kill him.

"You really didn't have my cabin searched while we were out today?" he asked.

She shook her head but then slowly added, "At least not intentionally..."

"But?"

"I might have asked one of my brothers to check into you," she said. "And they can be overly protective."

Alarm struck his heart. But his new identity was solid; Italian authorities had helped him with all the documentation. "Gideon?" He'd had time to search the cabin; he and Jasper had returned earlier than they had.

She shook her head. "I didn't ask Gideon to check into you. He's a social worker. I have other brothers. One of them is an FBI agent."

He shrugged as if it didn't matter. But it did...

How much could the FBI find out about him? Would just an inquiry alert the Camorra to where he was? He needed to leave the ranch, he knew—for his sake and most especially for hers. But there was something he needed to do first, a temptation he could no longer resist.

So he leaned down again and brushed his mouth across Aubrey's soft lips. And he braced himself for her to hurt him the way she had her ex-boyfriend.

But instead, she kissed him back, her lips moving

over and clinging to his. And Luca knew he was going to get hurt even worse than if she'd kneed him.

Dominic's phone rang—the cell for which only a select few people had the number. He had that device because he was about to go undercover again, and he couldn't take the other one, which might lead someone back to all the important contacts in his life: his family.

"Yeah?" he answered with his usual caution. He hadn't been given the new assignment yet. He was still doing the paperwork and interviews to wrap up the last one.

"Agent Colton?"

He recognized the voice of the supervisory special agent. "Yes, this is Colton."

"You've been asking around about someone…"

Around? He'd asked a couple of other agents, his international connections. "I made some inquiries about a Luke Bishop," he admitted. "I know I didn't have much to go on…" So he hadn't expected much, certainly not a call back from a bureau supervisor.

"There's one strong possibility for the Luke Bishop you're inquiring about," the supervisor said. "One guy who seems to have just materialized less than a year ago."

Dominic sucked in a breath, surprised that Aubrey's *feeling* about her mysterious guest had been right.

"What's your interest in this, Colton? Did you suspect that he could be on the wanted list?"

Dominic's pulse quickened. He sure as hell hoped Bishop wasn't on any such list, not when the man was staying at Gemini Ranch, and especially not when his sister seemed very curious about him. "Just checking him out over someone else's suspicions."

Maybe Aubrey should have gone into law enforcement—she obviously had good instincts. She had been hurt before, though, by that idiot Warren Parker. After that unfortunate experience, she was obviously being more cautious.

"Is he on the wanted listed?" Dominic asked.

"We won't know unless we figure out who he really is," the supervisor said. "It feels like this is a new identity. There's the possibility, I guess, that he could be in witness protection, but the US Marshals aren't usually very forthcoming with information about WITSEC."

Dominic knew one marshal who would be, especially when she learned that the information was for their sister. But he wasn't going to give up that connection to his supervisor.

"Can you forward me what you found?" Dominic asked. "I'll make some more queries."

"Let me know what you turn up."

"Of course," Dominic said. But his supervisor wouldn't be the first person he notified; his sister would be. Or maybe Jasper...

Because Aubrey would confront this Luke Bishop with whatever she learned—no matter how dangerous he might be—while Jasper would be cautious.

After disconnecting that call, Dominic picked up his other phone and called one of those personal contacts.

"Dominic, are you okay?" Alexa Colton answered, her voice full of concern. As a marshal, she knew how dangerous his job could be—which unsettled Dominic as much as it did her.

He didn't like that his baby sister had gone into a dangerous profession as well. "I'm fine," he assured her. "You?"

"Of course. I can take care of myself," Alexa replied, her voice sharp with defensiveness.

He hoped that she was right, that she could.

"Is that why you called?" she asked. "To check up on me?"

"No," he said. "I want you to check up on a man called Luke Bishop."

"Who's he?"

"That's what I would like to know. I'm going to forward you what's been dug up about him so far," he said. "I want to know if he's in WITSEC."

"I can't tell you if he is—"

"It's for Aubrey," he interrupted her protest. "She asked me to check him out."

"Why?"

"He's a guest at the ranch."

"Has she ever had you check out a guest before?" Alexa asked.

"No."

They both knew what that meant—that Aubrey was interested in this guy. Something was going on.

"Okay, send me what you have, and I'll let you know what I find out," she told him. "In the meantime, tell Aubrey to stay away from him. Even if he's in WITSEC, that doesn't mean he's one of the good guys. He could have just made a deal to flip on his partners to save himself some prison time."

"I know…" No matter who Luke Bishop was, his curiously new identity made him too dangerous for Aubrey to be around him.

Chapter 7

What the hell had she done?

Aubrey flopped around again on her bed, her body aching with longing. How had she sent Luke away after that kiss? How had she found the willpower to push him back and tell him it was time for him to leave?

She'd offered him the truck to drive back to his cabin, but he'd insisted he needed the cold air. And she had been able to imagine why—for the same reason she'd taken a cool shower after he left.

But still her skin had been hot with desire, her body tense with need. How had just a kiss affected her so much?

Because it hadn't been just a kiss. It had been like an explosion. The minute his mouth brushed across hers, the attraction that simmered between them had burst into a passion so hot and fierce that it had felt like a flashfire.

And she would have let it burn her alive in that moment...if she hadn't felt the vibration of her phone. Somebody had been calling or texting her, and that interruption had brought her back to her senses.

She'd suspected it was Warren, trying to whine and manipulate her into giving him that second chance and probably a significant loan. And that had reminded her of her poor judgment, that for some reason she was only attracted to men that she couldn't—or shouldn't—trust.

Maybe she had more daddy issues than she'd realized after what her father had done, the double life Ben Colton had led. All those thoughts had tumbled through her mind and doused that conflagration of desire like a bucket of ice water.

But even though she'd found the strength to send Luke away, she hadn't been able to stop thinking about him or to stop wanting him, and so she'd spent a restless night flopping around on her bed while outside the wind howled.

The storm was beginning to intensify. There wouldn't be much time to move the rest of the cattle. So at the first light of dawn, she gave up trying to sleep and jumped out of bed. She dressed quickly and skipped breakfast, her stomach still too unsettled to eat. But she packed some food, leftovers from the kitchen at the main lodge, into a backpack. She didn't need to worry about keeping any of it cold, not with how much the temperature had dropped. She slung the backpack over her shoulder and headed out to her truck. Once she'd brushed off the snow and warmed it up, she reached for her cell phone to let Jasper know she was heading to the barn. When she glanced at the screen, she saw that the call she'd missed the night before hadn't been from Warren but from Dominic.

Her pulse accelerated. Had the FBI agent found out something already about Luke? Had he been the one who'd searched her guest's cabin the day before? She'd thought he was in Denver, though, so maybe he'd enlisted Jasper or Gideon to carry out his orders.

Jasper would have been able to access the code for the lock on Luke's cabin as easily as she had. Or maybe the receptionist, knowing Gideon was her brother, had given him the code.

The woman also often stepped away from her desk without locking her computer, so anyone in the main lodge might have been able to access it—if they'd found her away from her desk.

Not that it mattered who'd searched it. Dominic must have found out something that he wanted to share with her. And she was stalling instead of calling him back...

She didn't want to know because she had a horrible feeling—like she'd had when her gaze had first locked with Luke's—that it wasn't going to be good. Otherwise, she doubted that Dominic would have sent a text reading:

Need to talk to you ASAP.

Cursing beneath her breath, Aubrey punched in Dominic's number. But she put the cell on speaker so that she could shift the truck into Reverse and back out of her driveway.

Despite the early hour, Dominic answered immediately and with obvious concern in his deep voice. "Where have you been?"

"Sleeping," she replied—even though it was a lie. She wished she'd been able to doze because today was going to be a long day. "Why'd you call so late?"

"Because you asked me to do you a favor," he reminded her.

"And you found out something about Luke…" He wouldn't have called had he not. Dread settled heavily in the pit of her empty stomach.

"Not really," he said. "There isn't much to find out about a man who just came into existence less than a year ago."

"What do you mean?" she asked. Luke had to be close to forty.

"That's as far back as he can be traced. Born in Naples to American parents, per his birth certificate and social security card, but…"

"So that means you've traced him back to his birth," she pointed out.

"Nope. No activity on that social security number with his date of birth until less than a year ago," Dominic said. "Your instincts were right. There's a whole lot to mistrust about this guy. He's obviously hiding something."

"Or maybe *he's* the one who's hiding," she murmured. That would explain his requesting the cabin farthest away from the main lodge, how he used all cash and made no calls but for maybe the ones on the cell phones he'd destroyed. She slowed the truck as she neared where Luke was staying.

"From what?" Dominic asked her. "From the authorities or from bad guys?"

She thought of how Luke had offered to help with the cattle, how hard he'd worked the day before, how he'd jumped to her defense last night with Warren and how when she'd pushed him away, he hadn't pressed her for more.

He'd respected her wish for him to leave. Unlike Warren, who kept trying to manipulate her into doing what he wanted.

I wish you could...

Maybe she had heard that correctly, what he'd replied when she'd assured him she would keep him alive while they moved the cattle.

"I would say he's hiding from bad guys," she said as she stopped beside his cabin.

"Why? Because he might have turned against them to save himself a prison sentence? Even if he's in witness relocation, that doesn't make him a good person," Dominic warned her. "You need to stay far away from him. Far, far away from him, Aubrey."

But just then the door to the cabin opened and Luke stepped out and walked toward the truck, getting closer and closer until he touched the handle. She hadn't unlocked it.

Yet. But she intended to. She intended to ignore her brother's advice because she suspected the only way to find out the truth about Luke Bishop was to stick close to him.

Very close...

"Thanks, Dominic," she said. And she clicked off the

cell just as he was starting to speak again. Then as she unlocked the passenger door, she powered off the phone.

She didn't want Dominic calling again or texting while she was with Luke. While her mysterious guest already knew she had her brother checking him out, she didn't want him to know what he'd found, or, actually, what he hadn't found.

A past…

Luke Bishop didn't have one. So who was he really?

While she'd unlocked the truck door for him that morning, Aubrey had locked Luca out in other ways. She'd barely spoken to him since she picked him up, and whenever he glanced at her, either in the barn or while riding, she wouldn't meet his gaze. It was as if she couldn't stand to look at him.

Maybe she was just intent on herding in the cattle. Or maybe she was embarrassed about what had happened the night before or could have happened had she not come to her senses. He should have been relieved that she had—because he'd been so overcome with desire that he hadn't been able to think at all, let alone rationally.

Realistically, he knew that he should leave—just in case that hadn't been one of her siblings who'd searched his cabin. Just in case the Camorra had somehow tracked him down once again…

And if one of its killers had…

Well, he wasn't willing to face that suspicion yet although it niggled at the edge of his consciousness, just as his desire for Aubrey niggled inside him, making him tense and edgy. Or maybe that was because he hadn't slept at all the night before.

He hadn't been able to stop tasting her on his lips, the sweetness of her mouth. He hadn't been able to stop feeling the heat and softness of her body pressed against his.

Despite the wind whipping around them, hurling sharp chunks of snow at their faces, heat flashed through Luca. Even though he knew she'd done the right thing last night when she pushed him away, he wished that she hadn't—that he could at least be with her once before he had to leave.

But that wouldn't be fair to her. Or to him—because it would make it even harder for him to say goodbye to her.

And the ranch…

He wasn't bored anymore. Moving cattle was hard work, especially with the storm coming at them full force now, but it was satisfying in a way nothing had satisfied him since filing his last exposé.

"Luke!" Aubrey called out, shouting over the roar of the wind.

And he tensed in his saddle at the alarm in her voice. "What is it?"

"Listen," she said.

They were moving the last of the livestock from a pasture near the mountains, its peaks now hidden by white. Only a few cows remained between him and Aubrey; he urged the last of them through the open fence.

She turned back, her head cocked as she listened. He couldn't hear anything over the wind. But she headed back, urging her horse in the wrong direction—into the swirling snow and the wind.

"Aubrey!" he yelled back at her. But she kept going. So he nudged his horse with his knees and followed her.

She stopped her horse and dismounted. The minute her boots hit the ground; she was crouching down—digging through a snowdrift.

He slid off his horse and squatted down next to her. "What are you doing?"

Then he heard it, too, the pitiful cry, so weak and soft…

How had Aubrey heard it? She used her gloves to wipe the ice off what he quickly realized was a small body: a calf.

There had been a few other calves, born early but healthy, among the cattle they'd moved, but not one like this, separated from the others.

Luca glanced around. "Where is its mother?"

She shrugged. "I don't know. Maybe we moved it yesterday…" Her voice cracked with emotion, with concern that they'd separated the baby from the dam. It was small, smaller than the other ones they'd found with their mothers in the herd yesterday. Maybe it had been born prematurely.

Many of the cows they were moving were about to give birth, which was yet another reason Aubrey had wanted them closer. So that if there were complications, she would be able to get a veterinarian to aid them.

Maybe there had been a complication with this birth and the dam had passed. He glanced around, looking for the mother while Aubrey moved her hands over the calf, trying to warm it. "We need to get it to the barn," she said.

He nodded. "We can head back now, keep the cattle moving that direction…"

He stood up then and turned toward his horse. He intended to climb into the saddle and have Aubrey hand him the calf. But when he closed his hands over the saddle horn, gunshots rang out.

The Camorra must have sent amateurs before him. Because Luca Rossi hadn't been nearly as hard to kill as he'd been warned that he was.

The only thing that was hard about this hit was the elements.

That damn snow fell so fast and hard now that he couldn't be entirely sure if Rossi was really dead or just injured and unable to move. But Rossi and that woman weren't the only ones in this area, so he couldn't risk getting close enough to check his body.

Somebody might see him. Like maybe that woman. He hadn't aimed at her. She'd been crouched on the ground, looking at something, so he hadn't worried about her seeing him. But if he got closer, she might.

Hell, she could even be armed because she was one of the property owners. The other one was out here somewhere, too, with other hands. The gunshots could bring them all riding over here.

So he had to leave now—before someone saw him. But he took one more look through the scope, to make sure, and he saw not one but two bodies, lying prostrate on the ground, not moving. Maybe he'd hit them both…

Chapter 8

Last night Aubrey had longed for this, to feel the weight of Luke Bishop's body lying atop hers. But she hadn't imagined those circumstances, that he would have knocked her flat onto her back on the cold, snow-covered ground.

"What the hell are you doing..." she murmured into his shoulder. She'd heard the shot, too. But it sounded like it had been a distance away, probably another ranch away.

But then she remembered Dominic's call and warning. Was someone after Luke Bishop? Had they killed him?

His body was heavy on hers, hard and unmoving. "Luke!" she exclaimed, gripping his shoulders now with her gloved hands, like she'd gripped the calf. It lay next to them, crying out weakly for its mother. "Are you all right?"

His hair brushed her cheek when he nodded. At least she hoped he nodded.

"Luke?" she asked again. "Are you sure?"

"Yes, I'm fine. Are you?" he asked, his breath warm against her cheek.

Her heart was beating fast and hard, and it was hard to breathe—either because of his weight pressed on top of her or because he'd knocked the wind out of her when he'd slammed her down so abruptly.

He braced his gloved hands beside her and levered himself up, but he remained crouched, glancing around as if he expected more shots to be fired.

She wasn't sure what to expect. Had someone purposely fired at them? And was that person out there yet? Then she heard the rumble of an engine. This far out from passable roads, it couldn't have been a vehicle; it must have been a snowmobile.

Luke must have heard it, too, because he stood up straight and peered around—as if trying to see through the snow. But the rumble was growing fainter as it drove away from them.

"Whoever it was who fired those shots must be leaving," she said, and she jumped up from the ground before the snow got her any colder. Like the poor calf…

She reached for it next, gathering it up in her arms again. "We need to get this little guy back to the barn before he freezes to death." And he probably wasn't going to be the only one.

"Are you really okay?" Luke asked, and from the gruffness of his voice, clearly he was not. The gunshots had shaken him up.

She was trembling, but she didn't know if that was from the cold or in reaction to those shots. "I don't think the bullets came anywhere near us," she said. "It must have been another rancher shooting at a coyote or a mountain lion." Her arms tightened around the calf. "Maybe that's what happened to this one's mama…"

Or, hopefully, they would find the dam already back at the ranch, in the pasture close to the indoor ring.

"We need to get back," Luke agreed as he swung his long body back onto his horse. Used to gunshots from hunters, their horses hadn't moved—hadn't reacted the way Luke had.

"Why did you react like that?" she asked. "Why would you assume someone was shooting at us? At you?" Who was he really?

He shrugged. "I think anyone who's lived in a big city knows to duck when you hear gunshots. It's instinct."

He hadn't just ducked, though. He'd knocked her flat and then covered her body with his, protecting her. Thinking first of her safety before his own.

He couldn't be the bad man her brother Dominic was worried that he was. No matter Luke Bishop's real identity, she doubted that he was a danger to her physically.

Now, emotionally…

He held out his arms. "Hand the calf up to me," he said. "I'll carry him back."

As Aubrey lifted the cold little animal, Luke opened his jacket and pulled the calf tight against his body— to keep it warm.

Her blood raced and she felt her face flush. And then Aubrey knew that Luke might just be a very serious threat to her heart.

Luca wasn't sure if Aubrey really believed that had just been another rancher firing at some threat to his livestock. He just knew that he didn't believe it. Those shots had sounded too close, too purposeful for him to think there had been anything innocent about them.

At least the snowmobile sounded as if it had driven away from them, not toward them. But that didn't mean that the shooter wasn't somewhere out there yet, between them and the barn—waiting to try for them again.

So Luke made certain to stick close to Aubrey as they drove the last of the livestock back toward the pastures closer to the barn. But with his arms wrapped around the weak calf, Luke wasn't sure how he would be able to protect Aubrey.

Or himself...

His arms strained from carrying the animal. Calves weren't born little: he knew that from his days of working on ranches, during his university breaks, in the Province of Isernia, not far from Naples. This one had to be close to eighty pounds, but Aubrey had managed to lift it up to him without much effort.

She was strong. He'd already known that. She was also fearless because she didn't seem as shaken as he was by their close call.

Or was it just that she hadn't realized how close it was?

With the wind blowing and the snow whipping around them, it was hard to hear—hard to see...

Yet she'd heard the calf and had found it in the snow. She was sharp, so sharp that he wondered maybe if he had overreacted. Maybe the shots hadn't been anywhere near them.

Maybe he hadn't endangered her life with his presence. Yet...

But he worried that the Camorra would find him, just as they had in the past. Someone had to be giving him up, betraying him.

"Luke!" Aubrey yelled.

And he tensed, worried that she'd heard something he hadn't again. Like the snowmobile...

"What?" he called back to her.

"Are you all right?"

He nodded.

"The calf isn't getting too heavy?"

He shook his head.

"We have a distance to go yet," she said, "and the weather is getting worse..."

The storm was definitely as bad as had been predicted. With his jacket open, he would have frozen, if not for the relative warmth of the animal cradled in his arms.

"Stick close," she told him. "It's getting to near whiteout conditions, and I don't want you to get lost."

While night was a few hours off, there wasn't much light shining through the sheets of snow falling on them. Maybe the shooter wasn't the worst danger right now.

Maybe the storm was...

The chandeliers, dangling from the rafters of the two-story great room, flickered as the power threatened to go out. If it did, the backup generators would kick on. They wouldn't be without electricity or heat at the main lodge.

Which was good since Jasper was still freezing. With the help of some ranch hands, he'd moved the last of the cattle from the pastures near the mountains. Aubrey and Luke had been working nearby, but the only people he'd seen, besides the other ranch hands, were some snowmobilers. A group of guests had gone on a guided excursion. But Jasper had been worried, with the storm intensifying, that the guests might get separated and into some trouble out there. So after putting away his horse, he'd hurried up to the main lodge to make sure they'd all returned safely.

Trisha, the snowmobiling guide, nodded, but then sheepishly admitted, "Several of them got separated from the main group for a while, but I made sure they all returned to the equipment shed. It was hard to see out there, and the snowmobiles just seemed to whip up the precipitation even more."

The young woman, a recent college grad with a degree in hospitality, stood beside Jasper in front of the giant stone fireplace. Her face was chafed from the cold like Jasper's probably was. His skin felt raw—at least what he could feel; he'd gotten so cold that he'd gone numb in some places.

"Did you hear the gunshots?" she asked.

Jasper tensed with concern. "Gunshots?" he echoed.

She nodded. "A few of the guests mentioned them. I thought I heard something, but with as loud as the machines are and then the wind…" She shrugged. "I'm not sure what it was…"

Gunshots?

Hunters weren't likely to be out during a blizzard, unless they weren't tracking animals…

He shook his head at the leap his imagination had taken to the worst-case scenario. The storm must have been getting to him.

The lights flickered again before going out. Some of the guests sitting in the great room gasped, while some chuckled. It was early evening yet, but night was close, so thick shadows darkened the lodge until the generators fired up.

He glanced around the room. Aubrey wasn't here. But then, she hadn't come up to the main lodge after getting back yesterday, either.

Maybe she had safely returned. But he needed to know for certain, so he grabbed his cell and tried calling her. But his phone stayed dead, the screen blank.

Either he'd run down the battery or lost a signal.

Probably both. So he walked over to the reception area and used a landline to call her house. The phone rang a few times before her voice mail picked up. He hung up before leaving a message, and then he called the extension in the barn.

"Gemini Ranch," Kayla answered the phone.

He recognized her voice, and his pulse quickened. But he was sure it was just with concern—for his twin. "Kayla, have you seen Aubrey?"

"No. I was going to wait for her to get back—"

"She's not back yet?"

"No." And now there was concern in her voice. "She and that guest—Luke Bishop—are both still out there."

He cursed. He should have checked on them while they were out in the storm, made sure they got back safely. If something had happened to her…

But he couldn't let his mind go there, either. Aubrey knew how to handle herself in any conditions.

"Do you want me to go out and look for them?" she asked.

"No!" he replied emphatically. "I don't want you getting lost out there."

"I would not get lost," Kayla replied, just as emphatically.

Maybe she wouldn't—she knew the ranch well. "I haven't been back that long, so I know how nasty it is out there," he said. "Don't go looking for them. I'm sure they're on their way back."

But what was taking them so long? Of course Aubrey had insisted that she would move the cattle from the pastures that were the farthest out. Jasper should have stood his ground, but he knew all too well that his twin usually won their arguments.

"Then I'll just wait and make sure they return safely," she said.

He looked out the windows at the snow swirling around the lodge in a thick white cloud. "No," he said. "You should get back to the bunkhouse or come up here to the main lodge. You don't want to get stranded out in the barn."

There was enough heat to keep the animals comfortable, but it wasn't warm enough for humans, except maybe in the tack room. But the small heater wasn't likely to warm the entire long room that was filled with saddles and other equipment.

"I'll go to my room in the bunkhouse," Kayla said.

"And be careful getting there," he advised. "It's pretty much whiteout conditions right now." Even the lights of the pickup truck wouldn't do much to help her see in this weather.

"I'll be fine," she said, her voice terse with defensiveness.

That was how his sister got, too, as if worrying about them meant that you didn't think they were as strong or tough as they were when all it really meant was that you cared…

Not that he cared about Kayla as anything other than an employee, but still he didn't want anything to happen to her.

She must have thought their conversation was over because she hung up on him. While he suspected Kayla could make it safely to the bunkhouse, he was worried about Aubrey and Luke, who'd been so far from the main buildings of the ranch.

Had they gotten lost out in the blizzard?

But Aubrey knew the ranch so well that she would have been able to make it back to the barn blindfolded.

But then another thought occurred to him…

What if the guests had been right? What if shots had been fired? And what if one of the bullets had struck Luke or Aubrey?

Then they could be out there, hurt and freezing.

Or worse…

Chapter 9

The wind hurled snow and ice against the barn as Aubrey fought to close the doors. Since Luke had been holding on to the calf, she was the one who'd jumped down from her horse to open the doors and to hold them open for him to enter with his burden. But when she'd jumped down, her body frozen from the cold, she'd nearly collapsed into the snow. But she'd managed and Luke had led her horse inside while he rode his and carried the calf. They were both in the barn now.

She continued her battle, the snow swirling through the doors and adding to the accumulation already on her hat and in her hair and scarf. But she couldn't quite get the doors shut. Then another body was there, pressing against the door beside her. With Luke's help, they shut and barred the entrance, and the wind outside seemed to howl even louder in protest.

Shaking with cold, she turned toward Luke and saw that he was shaking, too, his arms jerking even as they dangled at his sides.

"Are you okay?" she asked with concern, her voice hoarse from the cold.

He didn't reply, just nodded, and snow fell from the brim of his hat.

"Your arms…"

Because he'd held the calf all the way from the pasture to the barn, he must have been having muscles spasms in his arms now. He'd carried the animal the entire trip back without complaint, even refusing when Aubrey had offered to take a turn. She'd thought at the time that he might not have heard her—with the way the wind had been shrieking and how hard the snow had been falling. If they hadn't stayed close to each other, they all might have been lost. She wanted to throw her arms around him and hug him close and not just for warmth. But she resisted the temptation, knowing they had to take care of the animals.

"I'm okay," he insisted, then he turned away and headed down the wide aisle. He stepped around the saddles he'd taken from the horses while she'd been struggling to close the doors. The animals were in their stalls, where Kayla must have left them fresh food and hay. The blankets spread over them must have been Luke's doing. He continued past to the stall where he'd left the calf, lying on fresh hay. He dropped to his knees beside it and reached out, using his gloved hands to rub its snow-covered coat.

"I…" She had no words for how impressed she was, for how he'd gone above and beyond what she could have expected of a paid ranch hand, let alone one of their guests. "I…"

He turned toward her. "Are you okay?" he asked.

No. She wasn't. She was in trouble—real trouble with Luke Bishop. But she couldn't admit that to him, so she focused instead on the calf. "Just worried about this little guy…" And herself.

She bustled around, gathering supplies. Within minutes she had a bottle ready for the calf and a warm blanket and some feed. "Now that I see him in here, out of the blizzard, I think he's a little older than I initially did," she said with some relief.

"That's good," Luke murmured.

She continued talking, more to reassure herself than to explain anything he probably already knew. "I think his mother must have nursed him for at least a week or so. He's had his colostrum, so his immune system will have started. He's more likely to survive…"

But he wasn't moving yet. His eyes were closed now, maybe in deference to the snow earlier. Luke had rubbed the ice from the calf's face and from his coat while she was fixing the bottle and gathering the other supplies. She pressed the nipple of the bottle to the baby animal's lips. At first he didn't react, didn't move, and she worried that they might already be too late to save the little guy. But then he latched on and suckled, albeit weakly, on the bottle.

"He's definitely nursed before," Luke agreed, and his breath shuddered out in a sigh of relief.

The calf tried to nuzzle then against the bottle, knocking it from Aubrey's hand. She picked it up and held it again, and Luke's big hand wrapped around hers, helping her hold it.

They both wore gloves, so they weren't really touching—at least not skin to skin—but she was still affected.

Still so incredibly attracted to him...

Hell, after today, after he'd thrown his body across hers to protect her and then been so gentle with the calf...

She was *more* than attracted to him.

But she couldn't be. She shouldn't be...

Not after Dominic had warned her. With the limited activity under the Luke Bishop that Dom had found with her guest's approximate age and description, that was probably not even his real name. So who was he?

And why had he automatically assumed that those gunshots were meant for him?

Was someone trying to end his life? And why?

Because of what they'd done or because of what he'd done?

She couldn't believe that this man who'd protected her, who'd carried the calf through a blizzard, was a bad person. Even now, as he watched the calf nurse, his light blue eyes brimmed with concern and tenderness.

The animal slurped the last of the milk from the bottle and continued tugging at the nipple, making it squeak.

And Luke chuckled, a deep, throaty sound that made Aubrey's pulse quicken.

"I brought some calf starter, too," she said, and she pulled out the mixture of minerals and vitamins and ground oats, soybean meal, molasses and cracked corn. She poured some into her glove and held it out.

The calf must not have had any of the starter yet because he didn't sniff at it, didn't try to eat it, just swung his head back and forth as he searched around for more milk.

"You need this, too, little guy," she said, and she pressed her hand against his mouth.

His tongue swiped out and across her glove, taking some of the mixture into his mouth. Then he swiped at it again and again. And as he nibbled at the mixture and her glove, she giggled.

Then he began to push his hooves against the stall floor until his legs straightened and he stood up and stumbled toward her, nuzzling against her. And she laughed with relief.

Luke's chuckle echoed hers. "Look at him! He's going to be okay!"

Since she was sitting on the ground, the calf was in her face, so she couldn't see anything but the animal. But she wanted to look at Luke instead, so she poured more starter mix onto the floor. Then she turned toward Luke and threw her arms around his shoulders.

"Thank you! Thank you!" she exclaimed. "You saved him. You're amazing…" And he was—whoever the hell he was—he had to be a good man because he'd done this.

Luca closed his arms around her, his gloved hands clutching the back of her jacket. He wanted to hold on to her forever. But he knew that he couldn't.

That he would have to let her go. That he would have to leave her.

He wanted to believe, like she seemed to, that the shots that had been fired had been just another rancher protecting his cattle. He wanted to believe that so badly, so that he could stay, so that he could think he was safe yet and so was she.

He wanted to stay at Gemini Ranch with her as long as he could, wanted to spend time with her no matter where they were or what they were doing—even moving cattle during a blizzard.

And rescuing a calf...

His arms ached from carrying it all the way back, but his efforts had been worth it. To see the little guy start moving like he was...

And to witness Aubrey's joy over the success of their rescue...

And to feel it. Her happiness warmed him as if the sun was shining brightly on him, but instead of warming him from the outside in, she warmed him from the inside out. He'd been frozen for so long—even before they'd been out in that storm. He'd been emotionally reserved for years, not allowing himself to feel anything for anyone because he'd been too busy, too focused or in entirely too much danger.

That hadn't changed. The threat to his life had just increased.

So he forced himself to relax his fingers, to release the back of her jacket, and to ease away from her. She held on to his shoulders yet, and the way she stared at him, her eyes dilated, her face flushed...

He wanted to kiss her so badly, and he suspected she

wanted the same. But it wasn't fair to get any more involved with her—not when he couldn't be as open and
honest as she wanted him to be.

So he pulled away from her and stood up, saying,
"We should make sure the horses are okay now."

"Yes, of course," she hastily agreed, and she stood
up now, too. "They must be cold and wet yet." Her face
was still flushed, but he suspected it was with embarrassment now.

She probably thought he was rejecting her when it
was entirely the opposite. He wanted her so damn badly.
But even more than he desired her, he didn't want to
hurt her. And if those shots hadn't been just a rancher
firing at a coyote or mountain lion, then the Camorra
might have found him again.

He felt a sickening lurch of dread in his stomach
that had as much to do with fear as with acceptance.
He couldn't deny it any longer. He couldn't pass off
being tracked down in every city as just a coincidence
anymore.

He knew who had betrayed him.

* * *

He's missing...

That was the text that Paolo had received just moments ago. What did that mean?

That Luca had once again escaped before the
Camorra had caught up with him? Or that he was missing and presumed dead?

He needed to know. So he called the number that had
texted him. "So he's gone?" he asked.

"Presumably…"

"What does that mean? He left the dude ranch? Or that…?"

"I cannot say…"

Because they didn't trust Paolo? Did they think he was recording this call? That he was as reckless as his journalist cousin had been when he'd accumulated enough evidence to take down nearly the entire organization?

Unfortunately he hadn't taken down all of them. Some remained—like the man who spoke to Paolo now.

"A winter storm has moved into the area," the man said. "People are missing…"

People.

Luca…

"But even if there is survival, for now, because of the severity of the storm, there will be no escape…"

No escape this time. An ache spread through his chest. He knew what that meant.

If Luca wasn't already dead, he would be soon.

Chapter 10

Aubrey's face burned and not just because it was so chafed from the wind and the cold. It burned with humiliation. She had pretty much thrown herself at Luke, and he hadn't reacted—beyond that first hug where he'd clutched her so tightly as if he hadn't intended to let her go.

But he hadn't kissed her.

In fact, he seemed intent now on getting away from her. Maybe he was just tired and cold, though. Like the horses. They quickly tended to Ebony and her mare. Since Luke had already taken off their saddles, they rubbed down the animals' coats, then groomed their mounts and picked their hooves. The horses already had clean stalls with fresh water, feed and hay.

Kayla must have done this before she'd left for the evening. The barn was empty but for the animals and her and Luke, which made it feel eerie—like they were the only two people in the world.

A world Luke apparently didn't want to share with her, because once the animals were tended and the tack put away, he headed right for a side door. When he turned the handle, the wind propelled the door back into him, nearly knocking him to the ground. Snow blasted into the barn with all the force and fury of a tornado, and even though on this side of the barn there were exterior lights, it wasn't possible to see outside. Not through the snow.

She couldn't even see her truck. It had to be there. Kayla had her own vehicle; she wouldn't have taken Aubrey's. It was either buried under snow or the falling precipitation was just too thick, too impenetrable to see through.

Kind of like Luke…

She couldn't see through him to the secrets he was carrying like he'd carried that calf, his arms straining from the effort.

The snow blasted his face, knocking his hat from his head while it clung to his hair and lashes. He blinked, trying to see, then he pushed his shoulder against the door and shut and locked it.

Was he worried about someone forcing their way inside?

He'd been on edge even before those gunshots; he'd been on edge from someone searching his cabin. What had he been worried that they would find?

"It has to let up," Luke said between gasps for breath from his battle with the door.

"Seems like it's getting worse," she murmured. And she wasn't talking just about the storm.

She was thinking about her attraction to him. Even though she knew better, knew that she couldn't trust him, she wanted him.

"If it had been like this earlier…" She shuddered to think that they might not have made it back. She'd been worried about the animals, about the calf, but their lives had been in danger as well.

Had Jasper and his crew made it back? She pulled her cell phone from her pocket as she peered around the barn. The horse Jasper usually rode was warm in its stall. A small sigh of relief shuddered out of her lips.

Her twin must be safe. He was probably worried about her, though. She hadn't checked in with him yet, like they usually checked in with each other. Her phone was dead, the screen black. She didn't know if the lack of signal had completely run down the battery or if the cold had broken the cell.

"I don't suppose you have a phone," she murmured to Luke.

He shook his head.

Fortunately there was a landline in the tack room, so she hurried toward it. Before she stepped inside, she glanced back at Luke. He was still by the door, staring at it as if he was tempted to try again—to go out into that storm.

"It's not safe to leave," she said.

He was still turned toward the door, but she heard what he murmured beneath his breath. "It might not be safe to stay, either…"

Unlike last time, she wasn't going to let his cryptic comment go without questioning it. "What did you say?" she asked. Because it had been a mutter, just a rasp of his deep voice, so maybe she had misunderstood.

He turned toward her and shook his head. "Nothing…"

She narrowed her eyes and studied his face. The skin that wasn't covered with salt-and-pepper stubble was chafed red but for the dark circles beneath his eyes. He didn't look as if he'd slept any better than she had the night before. Or maybe he was just exhausted from the day. "You said something," she persisted. "Something about it not being safe to stay here…"

Instead of denying it again, he nodded. "I just meant that while the barn is warm enough for animals, it's probably too cold for humans."

"The tack room has a small wall heater," she said. And like the main lodge, there was a generator in case the power went out. She pushed open the door to the tack room and waited for him.

But Luke was clearly hesitant to join her. "I'll check on the calf again," he said.

"Thanks," she said. She stepped inside the tack room and reached for the phone on the wall. First she dialed Jasper's cell, but an automated message proclaimed that exchange unavailable. The blizzard was so fierce that it must have blocked reception from the cell tower.

She dialed the number for the main lodge. She suspected Jasper would be there, keeping the guests calm in case any of them were worried about the storm. "Gemini Ranch."

"Jasper," she said, recognizing his voice and surprised that he'd answered instead of one of the staff. He must have been waiting for a call.

"Aubrey, you're all right? You made it?" he asked.

"To the barn," she said. "We found an abandoned calf, so it took us longer to ride back."

"Is it okay?" he asked. "Are you okay?"

"Yes."

"I heard there were shots fired earlier."

She nearly groaned over his bringing them up. She'd wanted to forget about them. Mostly she'd wanted to forget Luke's reaction. "I'm sure it was nothing."

But she wasn't sure of anything or anyone…

"Just another rancher," she said. "Something must have happened to the mother of the calf we found, so maybe there's a mountain lion on the prowl or a coyote…"

Jasper released a shaky breath. "You're damn lucky you made it back. Are you really all right?"

"I'm fine," she assured him. Now she was the one lying, though, because she wasn't fine. She was rattled, but it had less to do with the storm and more to do with the man with whom she would have to ride out the bad weather.

"What about Luke Bishop?" he asked.

"He's fine, too," she said. "Just sore from carrying the calf in on his mount."

"We'll have to comp his stay," Jasper remarked. "He's worked hard."

"Yes, he has," she agreed.

"Though maybe we should wait and see how long he intends to stay before we give him the cabin for free," Jasper said with a chuckle.

How long *did* he intend to stay? Aubrey wondered. "I'll ask him," she said.

"Are you still together? He's in the tack room with you?"

"He's checking on the calf," she said. "But I'm not sure we'll be able to leave the barn. It's coming down even harder now."

"Whiteout conditions," he said. "Weather reports are saying to shelter in place."

"For how long?"

"At least until morning. There won't be a break until then," he said. "Do you want me to come out to get you?"

"If I can't see to drive away from here, how will you be able to see to drive to get here?" she asked him.

"I just don't like that you're out there alone," he said.

"I'm not alone," she reminded him.

"That's what I don't like about it most," he admitted.

Maybe Dominic had talked to him, had shared with him what he'd learned—or actually hadn't been able to learn—about Luke Bishop.

"Don't worry," she told him. "I will be fine." Just a short while ago, Luke had been the one who'd pulled away from her.

He hadn't kissed her like she'd wanted him to, like he had the night before when he'd come to her house. He'd left then, when she'd pulled away. He would respect her wishes.

She didn't need to worry about unwanted attention from Luke Bishop She needed to worry about how much of himself he was holding back from her.

Like his real identity...

* * *

The calf was asleep, peacefully, and warm in its bed of straw, a barn cat—a tiger-striped gray tabby—curled up at its side. Luca petted them both and considered staying there, in the straw with them. But his stomach rumbled; he wasn't just cold but also hungry.

He and Aubrey hadn't stopped once that day to eat. It had been too important to round up the cattle. But now he was a little light-headed and shaky from low blood sugar. He needed something. So he left the animals in the stall and headed to the tack room where Aubrey was.

He heard the soft sound of her voice and hesitated a moment. She was talking to someone. Had another person returned to the barn?

But he didn't hear anyone else speaking. So he pushed open the door, wondering if she'd been talking to herself. She cradled a phone against her shoulder while she foraged in the backpack she'd placed on one of the tables in the long room. The air was warmer in here and rich with the scent of leather and polish.

"I'm fine," Aubrey said, her voice sharp with frustration. "Stop worrying about me, Jasper, and tend to the guests. You need to make sure the generator stays running. We can't have any guests freezing to death." Then she pulled the receiver away from her ear, her brother's voice still emanating from the speaker, and hung it up on the cradle.

"What about starving?" Luca asked. "Are you going to let any guests starve to death?"

She gestured at the containers she'd spread out on the table. "I intended to share," she told him.

He should have packed something for himself, but

the supplies he'd ordered from town had gotten low. He was going to need to order more if he intended to stay.

But he didn't, he couldn't…

Even as longing pulled at him, at his heart, at his stomach…

It growled, and Aubrey giggled, like she had over the cattle. And something kicked his heart, making it beat harder. And suddenly he wasn't hungry just for food but for her as well.

So damn hungry…

She leaned toward him…with one of the containers. "Think it might be a little frozen yet from being outside with us," she said. "But there's a microwave in the corner over there." She gestured past boot-filled cubbies toward a small refrigerator with a microwave sitting on top of it.

Luca took the container from her, picked up a couple of other ones and carried them toward the microwave.

"You're going to share, too?" she asked.

He chuckled. "I'll bring them back." Then he teased, "Empty…"

"I have the silverware," she said.

"Who needs silverware?"

She chuckled again.

And some of the tension inside Luca eased. He heated up the dishes and brought them back to the table. They pulled up chairs on either side of it and feasted on their dinner of beef stew, roasted vegetables, a cheesy noodle dish and some kind of breaded meat.

Even as he filled his stomach, it rumbled. This time in appreciation. "You're an excellent cook," he complimented her.

She shook her head. "I can't claim credit for this meal. This is all the work of the brilliant chef we have at the main lodge. I don't cook. I know my limitations, unlike my mom, who keeps trying." Her lips curved into a warm smile at the mention of her mother.

"You're close to your mom," he said.

She nodded, but her smile was a bit more wistful now. "As close as you can be when you're one of a dozen kids that she basically raised on her own. I admire her, but I've always had to share her. That's one perk you had, being an only child. You never had to share."

"No, I didn't have to," he agreed. His heart ached with missing his mother. When he'd left her, he'd explained why he'd had to stay away. He'd even sent her off on her own adventure, on a cruise with her sister, Paolo's mother.

"She must miss you," Aubrey said.

And that pang in his chest intensified. He dropped the spoon he'd been holding into one of the empty containers. "Maybe while we were eating, the storm let up…"

Her smile slipped completely away, and she shook her head. "No, Jasper said there's not going to be a break until morning."

"A break?"

"A cold air system that's going to hover for a bit," she said. "Authorities are advising no travel for a few days yet."

A few days.

So if an assassin hired by the Camorra had fired those shots, Luca was stuck on the ranch with them. The tension was back inside him, gripping him so tightly that he struggled to breathe.

She must have noticed his reaction to her news because she asked, "Were you intending to travel?"

He shook his head.

"How long will you stay at the ranch?" she asked.

He shrugged. "I haven't made any plans." His only plan was to stay alive, and to do that, he had to stay at least one step ahead of the Camorra.

"What about your book?" she asked. "Are you really writing one?"

"You think I've lied about that?" he asked.

"I think you're not being completely honest with me," she said.

"Do you ever think anyone's being completely honest with you? Or did your dad and Warren destroy your ability to trust?"

She sucked in a breath, and Luca worried that he'd gone too far.

"I'm not criticizing you," he assured her. Then he uttered a heavy sigh. "In fact, I should be commending you. You're smart not to trust anyone." And maybe if he'd been that smart, he wouldn't have to be worried that he'd been found again.

But if he had…

Then there was no denying that only one person could have given him up—someone he had believed he could trust. Someone he loved like a brother.

"Sounds like you might have trusted someone you shouldn't have as well," she surmised. "Is that why you're hiding out here? Why you're traveling under an assumed name?"

He sucked in the breath now. "Assumed name? Is that what your brother told you?" he asked, and his heart pounded fast and hard with nerves.

He'd thought his new identity had been so well established. Maybe he shouldn't have trusted the people who'd helped him create it, either. After discovering how many people the Camorra had corrupted in the government and law enforcement, Luca hadn't entirely trusted them before he wrote his exposé. And he definitely didn't trust them not to betray his true identity now. That was why he always paid with cash instead of using credit cards.

Instead of answering her, Aubrey just silently studied his face, her blue eyes narrowed with suspicion.

"Your FBI agent brother thinks he's found something," Luca surmised now.

"No," she said. "He wasn't able to find out much of anything about you. That's why he's worried."

"Are you?" Luca wondered. What did she think he was—a criminal on the run? He wanted to tell her everything, but if the Camorra had already sent someone here…

Then that person might hurt her, too, if they figured she knew too much. It was safer for her to know nothing or as little as possible about him. Unfortunately he'd probably already revealed too much about himself, but he'd never felt as comfortable with anyone else as he did her. As connected to anyone else…

They were so different, but yet he felt as if he knew her on some other level. Was this connection what people were feeling when they spoke of soul mates? He'd always thought that was overly romantic drivel, some-

Get ready to relax and indulge with your FREE BOOKS and more!

Claim up to FOUR NEW BOOKS & TWO MYSTERY GIFTS – absolutely FREE!

Dear Reader,

We both know life can be difficult at times. That's why it's important to treat yourself so you can relax and recharge once in a while.

And I'd like to help you do this by sending you this amazing offer of up to FOUR brand new full length FREE BOOKS that WE pay for.

This is everything I have ready to send to you right now:

Try **Harlequin® Romantic Suspense** books featuring heart-racing page-turners with unexpected plot twists and irresistible chemistry that will keep you guessing to the very end.

Try **Harlequin Intrigue® Larger-Print** books featuring action-packed stories that will keep you on the edge of your seat. Solve the crime and deliver justice at all costs.
Or **TRY BOTH!**

All we ask in return is that you answer 4 simple questions on the attached Treat Yourself survey. You'll get **Two Free Books** and **Two Mystery Gifts** from each series you try, *altogether worth over $20*! Who could pass up a deal like that?

Sincerely,

Pam Powers

Harlequin Reader Service

Treat Yourself to Free Books and Free Gifts.

Answer 4 fun questions and get rewarded.

We love to connect with our readers! Please tell us a little about you...

	YES	NO
1. I LOVE reading a good book.	◯	◯
2. I indulge and "treat" myself often.	◯	◯
3. I love getting FREE things.	◯	◯
4. Reading is one of my favorite activities.	◯	◯

TREAT YOURSELF • Pick your 2 Free Books...

Yes! Please send me my Free Books from each series I select and Free Mystery Gifts. I understand that I am under no obligation to buy anything, as explained on the back of this card.

Which do you prefer?

❏ **Harlequin® Romantic Suspense** 240/340 HDL GRCZ
❏ **Harlequin Intrigue® Larger-Print** 199/399 HDL GRCZ
❏ **Try Both** 240/340 & 199/399 HDL GRDD

FIRST NAME   LAST NAME

ADDRESS

APT.#   CITY

STATE/PROV.   ZIP/POSTAL CODE

EMAIL ❏ Please check this box if you would like to receive newsletters and promotional emails from Harlequin Enterprises ULC and its affiliates. You can unsubscribe anytime.

HI/HRS-520-TY22

thing to explain the way friends had dropped him to spend all their time with their new significant other.

"I should be worried," she said.

"I am," he admitted. He was worried about these feelings. But most of all he was worried about leaving her without learning more about her: like how she would feel when they made love, how she would make him feel…

He suspected that because of the connection they shared, it would be an experience beyond anything he'd ever felt before.

He didn't dare share those thoughts with her, though, just as he didn't dare share anything else. But he couldn't help grinning and teasing her, "You should be worried…"

"Are you dangerous?" she asked.

He didn't want her to be afraid of him, to think that he was a bad person, and the urge to tell her everything overwhelmed him. But he just shook his head and said, "Maybe dangerous to be around…"

"Why?" she asked.

Wanting to keep her safe but also share more with her, he began, "Let's just say in doing research…"

"For your book?" she asked when he trailed off.

Maybe he could be honest about that, although he hadn't intended to write a book when he'd first started investigating. But then he'd uncovered so much…

"Yes," he replied, "the research I did for the book has brought me to some dangerous places with some dangerous people."

"But you said you're writing fiction," she said. "Did you lie to me?"

"Calling it fiction protects me," he said. And believing it was fiction might have kept her safe, had she been able to read any of his notes.

After he'd caught her snooping around his kitchen, he'd hidden his laptop, notebook and those destroyed phones. And it hadn't appeared that the intruder had found his hiding spot in the empty space beneath the bottom drawer of the chest of drawers in the bedroom. He'd already been hiding the documents for his new identity there—the passport and credit cards.

"What does calling it fiction protect you from? Lawsuits or from these dangerous people hurting you?" she asked. "Is that why you're hiding out?"

He wondered now if she was the journalist and he was the rancher. She was a natural at interviewing, but he just smiled at her instead of answering her question. Then he leaned across the table, until his face was close to hers, and said, "I think I'm in more danger here— with you—than I've been anywhere else…"

And not just because the Camorra might have found him.

"Why?" she asked.

"Because you are a dangerous woman, Aubrey Colton," he said. A woman who tempted him to share all his secrets, to share everything with her—even his heart.

If only it was safe for him to stay, then maybe he'd follow his heart when it fell…for her.

The cell phone vibrated across the nightstand next to Dominic's bed. He swiped to accept the call and answered with a gruff hello.

"Did I wake you up?" Alexa asked.

He sighed, wishing she had. "No…"

He needed to get some rest before his next assignment started. When he was undercover, he could never completely relax. Never let his guard down…

Sometimes his life depended on staying awake and aware. So he saved his sleeping for when he was between assignments.

But now he was so on edge about Aubrey's mysterious guest that he couldn't sleep.

"What did you find out?" Dominic asked his US marshal sister.

Alexa exhaled a sigh, a ragged one of pure frustration. "I wasn't able to find him in WITSEC, so he's not with the US Marshals."

"Or with Federal," Dominic said. "Aubrey said he has some kind of European accent. He might be Italian, since his documents, doctored or not, claim that's where he was born."

Alexa sighed. "I don't have any overseas connections."

"I already checked with mine," Dominic said. "Maybe Ezra can check with his."

Their brother Ezra, one of Dominic's fellow triplets, was a US Army sergeant, but sometimes Dominic suspected he was something more. He was harder than hell to reach, though.

"Good luck getting a hold of him," Alexa said. "In the meantime, you need to tell Aubrey to steer clear of the guy."

"I already have. Maybe you should talk to her," Dominic suggested. Aubrey was strong and stubborn. Too stubborn to admit that she wasn't that tough when it came to matters of her heart.

Alexa chuckled. "Ah, no. I'm your baby sister," she reminded him, even though she and her twin, Naomi, actually shared that title.

"Afraid of Aubrey?" he teased her.

"I respect her," she said. "And I know what it's like when people don't think you can take care of yourself."

It hadn't been easy for Alexa to become a US marshal, and the hardest part for her had probably been her family trying to discourage her from joining the organization, out of their concern that she would be hurt.

"Okay," he said with a weary groan. "Point taken. I'll call Jasper."

Alexa groaned, too. "You guys just don't get it," she complained. "Your sisters, including me, can take care of ourselves."

In his head he knew that; he knew they were all so strong and smart—like Mom. But in his heart he loved them too much to do nothing when he thought one of them might be in danger.

Alexa willingly put herself in the line of fire for her job—so he usually worried about her the most. But Aubrey...

She wouldn't have asked Dominic to check out her guest if she wasn't interested and concerned about the mysterious Luke Bishop. And she'd already had her heart and ego hurt once by a man she shouldn't have trusted...

Twice, if you counted Dad. And Dominic tried not to think about him, about any of that. He focused only on the things he could change or help. And he was too far away to help Aubrey right now, especially with the storm that had struck Denver and the surrounding areas. So, after hanging up from Alexa, he called Jasper.

Or he tried. The first call—to his cell—didn't go through, so he called the main number for Gemini Ranch and asked for him.

He must have been at the lodge because within seconds, Jasper was on the line. "What's up, Dom?" Jasper asked.

"Everything okay there?" Dominic asked.

"You heard about the storm?"

"It hit here, too," Dominic said. "I'm just calling to make sure everyone's all right."

"I'm fine…" Jasper murmured.

"What about Aubrey? Is she with you?"

"She's spending the night in the barn," Jasper said. "Got stuck out there after bringing back the cattle."

Dominic sucked in a breath from a jab of concern. "Won't she freeze?"

"There's a heater in the tack room and a generator to keep it running if the power goes out again."

"Again?"

A ripple of noise emanated from Dom's cell; it must have been the collective gasp of the guests.

"Again," Jasper confirmed. "It keeps blinking on and off and off…" He sighed. "But the generator kicks in, so we're good. How's everyone else?"

"Everyone else?" Dominic asked. Even though he was one of the triplets, he felt like a loner most of the time. He and his brothers stayed connected, aware of where each other was or what was going on, but they each lived pretty solitary lives.

"You said you were checking on everyone," Jasper reminded him. Then he added, "Or are you just checking on Aubrey? What's up?"

"She asked me to look into a guest for her," Dominic admitted. "You didn't know?" If she hadn't shared her suspicions with her twin, something was definitely up.

"Luke Bishop?" Jasper asked.

"Yes." So maybe he had known.

Jasper cursed.

"What? What is it?"

"Did you find out anything bad?" Jasper asked. "What did you learn?"

"Just that she was smart to be suspicious," Dominic admitted. "There's something not right about the guy. Why? What do you know about him?"

"That he's with her in the barn right now," Jasper said. "He got stuck out there with her."

So Aubrey was trapped alone with a man she didn't trust.

A man who shouldn't be trusted...

Dominic cursed now.

"He doesn't seem like a bad guy, though," Jasper said.

But he tended to see the positive in life instead of the reality.

"He's been helping us move the cattle," Jasper said. "He's a hard worker."

That didn't make him a good person. Dominic had known some really hardworking criminals through the years he'd been a federal agent. And then there was another criminal he'd known well... That he and his siblings had all known well. A seemingly hardworking judge who'd turned out to be a criminal.

"Just keep checking on her," Dominic urged him. "Make sure that she's safe."

"Aubrey is tough," Jasper said. "She got through the blizzard. And earlier…"

"What?" Dominic asked when his brother trailed off.

"Earlier there were some shots fired."

"At Aubrey?"

"She didn't think so. A cow is missing. A calf abandoned. She thinks someone was probably shooting at a mountain lion or coyotes…"

Or Luke Bishop and whoever was unfortunate enough to be too close to him.

Like Aubrey…

Panic gripped him. He didn't want his sister getting caught in the crossfire between Luke Bishop and whoever might have tracked him down. Dominic didn't know yet who the man really was, but maybe someone else had figured it out, someone who might have wanted him dead.

Dominic wedged his fingers between the blinds on his bedroom window and peered out. The streetlamp was only a faint glow through the heavily falling snow, and he couldn't even see the road. It hadn't been plowed; interstates were getting shut down. He was trapped here—unable to help his sister—while she was trapped with Luke Bishop.

Whoever the hell he was…

Chapter 11

More than the table between them separated Aubrey and Luke.

She didn't believe for a moment that the book he was writing was fiction—if he was even writing anything at all. She doubted that Luke Bishop—or whoever he really was—had been honest with her about anything. Yet she still wanted him...

What was wrong with her?

Why was she only attracted to men that she couldn't—that she *shouldn't*—trust?

"We should check on the calf again," Luke said. "Maybe bring him in here with us if he's not warm enough."

Aubrey was warm now, the warmth spreading from her heart. He'd been so sweet with that calf, so protective and as determined to rescue it as she had been.

"I'll bring it another bottle," she said. While Luke cleaned up the containers from their belated dinner, she retrieved the milk from the small refrigerator.

He opened the door and held it for her, and as she passed him, her pulse quickened. She drew in a deep breath of his scent. He smelled like hay and horses and fresh snow and man. She was hesitant to release the breath, wanting to hold the smell inside her for just a bit…until she found the strength to come to her senses.

To avoid temptation…

But that was beginning to prove harder and harder, especially when she knew they were trapped in the barn. The snow was still blowing so hard outside that some of it had filtered through the small crack beneath the big double doors, forming a drift just inside the barn.

She shivered as the cold swirled around them, and Luke's arm moved over her shoulders, pulling her tight against his side.

"Are the animals going to be warm enough?" he asked.

She nodded. "The bigger animals like cattle and horses can survive frigid temperatures, and despite the ferocity of this storm, it's just a little below freezing. The barn is warmer than that, though, and has a ventilation system that keeps warmth circulating with drier air."

"So they'll all be okay?" he asked. "Even the little guy and the cat?"

"Cat?" Aubrey asked.

Luke pulled open the door of the stall where they'd settled the calf, and she saw the gray tabby curled up against the calf. "Isn't it sweet?" Luke asked, and he stepped away from her to kneel next to the animals. "The cat is taking care of our new friend."

She chuckled. "More like taking advantage of his body heat."

"You're so cynical," Luke remarked, but he grinned at her when he said it.

Aubrey felt the pang of regret nonetheless. "How are you not?" she asked as she knelt down next to him.

He stared down at her, deep into her eyes, and said, "Because I've met some pretty amazing people over the years."

Was he talking about her?

"That's why you think someone's searching your cabin and that those shots today were meant for you? Because you've met *amazing* people?" she asked, reminding him of the things he'd said.

His grin slipped away, and he sighed. "I've met some amazingly bad people, sure. I've also met some amazingly good people." And his hand covered hers over the bottle of milk. They'd removed their gloves in the tack room and must have left them there. His skin wasn't cold, though, and the touch of it—his touch—warmed hers. Just being close to him had heat streaking inside her as her blood pumped fast and hard.

She pressed the bottle into his hand and said, "You can feed him."

The calf nuzzled the bottle, then slurped greedily from it. The cat lapped up the drips that fell from the calf's chin.

Luke chuckled. "You might be right. She is a little opportunist."

Aubrey stroked her hand over the cat's head. "She

looks well-fed. Somebody's been taking care of her here." Aubrey hadn't seen her before, but the feline must have belonged to one of the ranch hands.

"And she's not the least bit skittish," Luke said as the cat pushed its head against Aubrey's hand and purred.

The calf greedily finished the bottle, then settled back into the pile of straw. The cat burrowed in next to it, and they closed their eyes, warm and content with each other's companionship.

"I guess they're fine," Luke mused.

"Yes," Aubrey agreed.

Luke shivered and said, "Now, I, on the other hand, would appreciate a little more heat. Unless…" He turned toward her and arched a brow. "I think you once offered to keep me warm…"

Aubrey snorted. "I was just making sure your furnace was working," she said, hanging on to the excuse she'd given him when he'd caught her in his cabin.

And she'd caught him fresh from the shower, his chest bare, the towel knotted just below his waist. Her heart was pounding so hard now, as she remembered seeing him like that, that she was surprised that he couldn't hear it, too.

Embarrassed and so very tempted to reach out to him, she jumped to her feet and hurried out of the close confines of the stall. "I—I should make sure the heater is working in the tack room," she said. "Or it's going to be a cold night."

Even though she hurried back to the tack room, Luke, with his long strides, easily caught up to her at the door. His hand covered hers on the knob as she reached out to turn it.

"I'll keep you warm," he offered, his voice a deep rumble near her ear.

Just the sound of it, and the heat of his breath in her hair, had her tingling everywhere. "Luke…" she murmured. She wanted him so badly.

Would it matter if she couldn't trust him as long as she knew not to fall for him? Could she just take tonight to appreciate and celebrate that they'd made it through a blizzard, that they were alive?

Especially if those shots hadn't been meant for wildlife but for…

Luke.

Could his life be in danger?

And if it was, she knew he wasn't staying. Hell, he was just a guest. And if he left without her knowing how it could have been between them, she would always wonder…

She turned toward him then and studied his face—his impossibly handsome face with its salt-and-pepper stubble clinging to the strong line of his jaw. "Are you married?"

His eyes widened in shock.

And she laughed at his expression of horror. "I'm not proposing," she assured him. "I just need to know." While it was bad enough that he was a guest, she couldn't break her personal rule and bend her moral principles—no matter how attracted she was to Luke.

He shook his head. "I've never even been close," he admitted as if he'd just realized that himself.

Men lied about being married all the time; she knew that, but something about the way he'd said it made her trust that it was the truth—probably more than anything else he'd told her.

So she turned the knob and pushed open the door. After she stepped inside, she reached back for him, grabbed the front of his jacket and tugged him toward her.

He reached for her, but his hands just cupped her shoulders and he stared down at her as he asked, "Are you sure?"

He knew then what she wanted, that she wanted him. She smiled and nodded. "Yes…"

"But—"

She reached up and pressed her fingers over his mouth. "You said you're not married. Were you lying?"

He shook his head.

Then she rose up on tiptoe and replaced her fingers with her mouth, sliding her lips over his. He stepped farther into the room then, his body pressing against hers, and he kicked the door shut with the heel of his boot.

He kissed her with a passion that equaled, if not surpassed, the desire she felt for him. His mouth moved hungrily over hers, his lips nibbling at hers, and then he deepened the contact even more, his tongue sliding over hers.

He kissed her as if he couldn't get enough of her until they finally broke apart, panting for breath. Her lungs burned with the need for air as her body burned with desire for his.

She couldn't remember ever wanting anyone this much. The passion coursing through her overwhelmed her. But even with him breathing heavy, too, she wondered if he wanted her as much…

She blinked away the haze of desire and focused on his face, which was flushed. His eyes were dilated. She'd been worried earlier, after Luke had pulled away when she hugged him out of gratitude over rescuing the calf, that he might not be as attracted to her as she was to him. Maybe she'd let Warren's manipulations affect her self-esteem, or maybe how much she was drawn to Luke had made her vulnerable, reminding her of the teased kid she'd once been.

She had survived school, though, and her regretful dating experience with Warren, and she would survive, too, when Luke checked out of Gemini Ranch, as he inevitably would.

But in the meantime…

She intended to make the most of this night with him. She pushed his sheepskin-lined coat from his shoulders and reached for the buttons of his blue flannel shirt. But his hands gently gripped hers, stopping her. "Too cold?" she asked.

"Too hot," he said, his voice gruff with passion. "I need to slow down. I need to take care of you first."

"Luke…" She was ready for him now.

But her hands clasped yet in his, he led her to one of the benches across from the boot cubbies, and he gently pushed her onto it before kneeling in front of it.

Nerves fluttered in her stomach now. It was almost as if he was proposing…and she knew that would never happen, but her heart…

She drew in a shaky breath and then murmured, "What are you doing?"

"Undressing you," he replied. First he tugged off one

of her boots. Her sock came with it, leaving her foot bare and cold. He rubbed it in his hands, warming it.

Warming her...

Heat trailed up from the arch of her foot his hand was massaging to her very core. "Luke..."

He tugged off the other boot and warmed that foot, too, until her toes curled in anticipation of what was to come. Of how he would make her feel when he touched her other places...

She looped her arms around his neck and pulled him toward her for another kiss. Lips nibbled on lips, tongues stroked and mated...

Then he broke away again with a low groan. "Aubrey..."

"I'm ready," she assured him. And she reached for the buttons of his shirt again.

But he ignored her efforts as he pushed her coat from her shoulders. It dropped onto the bench behind her. Then, as she clumsily fumbled with the buttons on his shirt, he deftly undid hers. His fingers brushed over every inch of skin he exposed.

She could barely breathe again and it wasn't from his kisses; it was from anticipation. She was so affected by just the sight of him, the taste of him on her lips...

Then his lips brushed across her mouth and slid down her throat and over her cleavage. He released the hook of her bra, and her full breasts burst out of the cups.

He groaned. "You are so beautiful, so incredibly beautiful..."

And the way he stared at her, as if in awe, made her

feel more beautiful than she'd ever felt. She felt more powerful than she'd ever felt.

Then his tongue swiped across one of her nipples, and she felt powerless, unable to stop the pleasure rushing through her. Not that she wanted it to stop; she never wanted it to stop. And that was the problem, that she was never going to want this feeling to go away.

His lips tugged at her nipple now, and she moaned as desire wound through her, twisting her stomach, making her ache for a release. "Luke…" Her hands slipped away from his shirt, from the buttons her fingers had been shaking too hard to undo.

His weren't shaking because he had no problem unbuttoning her jeans. Once he unzipped them, he tugged the worn denim down her legs along with her panties. Then with his mouth and those steady fingers, he took care of her like he'd promised, finally releasing that unbearable pressure he'd built inside her.

Clutching his shoulders, she screamed his name as the power of the orgasm overwhelmed her. "Luke!"

She couldn't remember any other lover being as generous, as unselfish. Hell, in that moment, she couldn't remember any other lover but Luke.

Her body pulsating yet with the pleasure he'd just given her, she should have been satiated. And she was, but she was also greedy for more. For all of Luke…

Desperate to see him again as she had that day in his cabin, when she'd been caught snooping, she returned her attention to his buttons again. She quickly undid them and then tugged up the thermal shirt he wore beneath his flannel. His abdominal muscles rippled as he helped shuck the shirt over his head.

She leaned forward and kissed his chest, swirling her tongue around one of his nipples. He groaned and then bucked as he rid himself of his jeans and underwear, as desperate now as she had been. Beneath her lips, his heart pounded hard. Then she skimmed her lips down his stomach, and those muscles rippled again. But then something else caught her attention…

He was so big. So engorged.

When she wrapped her fingers around his pulsating shaft, he groaned as if in pain. Then his hand covered hers, stilling it. With his other hand, he rifled through their discarded clothes until he found a condom packet. His hands were shaking too badly now, so she took the packet from him and tore it open. Then she rolled the condom over him. He pulsated within her hand and groaned again.

"Aubrey…"

Despite the cool air in the tack room, sweat beaded on his brow, on his lip. "I'm so on edge… I can't…"

She pushed him back on the floor, on top of the clothes they'd discarded there. And she straddled him, guiding him inside her. She could only take so much of him—he was that big. But she moved her hips, arching, taking him as deep as she could.

He moved within her, thrusting, as he gripped her hips, guiding her up and down. They found a rhythm together, as if they were dancing, as if it was a step they'd done many times.

She bit her lip and moaned as the pressure built again. Then he drove deeper inside her, and that pressure snapped. She screamed again as an orgasm shuddered through her.

Then he shouted her name, as his body convulsed beneath her with the power of his release. She collapsed onto his chest, which heaved with his deep breaths and the mad pounding of his heart.

Her heart pounded, too—from the exertion and from panic. Because she'd thought she could just enjoy the moment, just appreciate being with him this once...

But it was too good. He was too good, and she knew she would want more, probably more than he was able to give.

His honesty and his love.

The storm had struck hard—in the tack room. And it had raged all night. Luca lay limp in the aftermath of it.

Clothes were strewn all around the room. At one point they'd managed to pull out some blankets and they'd made a makeshift bed. They lay in it now, Aubrey curled against his side, her head on his chest.

She was so warm, so soft and comfortable in his arms, like she belonged there. Like Luca belonged here...

If only that was possible, if only he could stay.

But he couldn't risk that the Camorra wouldn't find him, if they hadn't already. He couldn't risk Aubrey getting hurt because of him.

But would she get hurt anyway? Was she getting as attached to him as he was to her?

Luca had never felt so close to anyone before. He hadn't lied when he'd told her he'd never even come close to getting married.

He'd always thought he was too busy before, but now he realized it was because he'd never found someone like her, someone who engaged him on every level. Someone who fascinated him as much as an interesting story had. Or maybe more…

Maybe that was because Aubrey had an interesting story of her own, with her father's betrayal, with her running a ranch.

She was a strong, incredible woman.

He'd thought he was satiated moments ago, but now his body began to stir again from the closeness of hers. Her hand was on his chest, over his heart, and maybe she'd felt it, felt the sudden increase in the beat because she chuckled—a low, sexy chuckle.

"Luke…" she murmured—so much quieter than when she'd screamed his name a short while ago.

He wanted to tell her his real name. Wanted her to scream "Luca" with all the wonder and pleasure that she'd screamed "Luke."

But he didn't dare share his real identity with her, especially if the Camorra was here. If she slipped up, if she called him Luca…

Then she might become the target he was.

He didn't want anyone getting hurt because of him, but most especially not her. He wanted to give her only pleasure.

Not pain…

He rolled then, onto his side, so she flopped onto her back. And he set about giving her more pleasure…

From a deep, drunken slumber, he was jerked awake—literally—as two men dragged him from his bed. His body struck the hardwood floor, pain shooting from his elbow down to his fingers. He didn't fight back. Did nothing to protect himself…

Just as he'd done nothing to protect Luca. He should have warned him. Instead, he'd betrayed him. But the Camorra had given him no choice. It was his life or Luca's.

And now he was going to die anyways. He'd been a fool—such a damn fool for getting involved with them in the first place. "What—what's going on?" he asked in Italian.

"That is what you need to find out," he was told. "There has been no confirmation from the assassins. You need to find out if your cousin is alive or dead."

"Uh, how?" he asked in confusion as he lay on the floor where they'd dumped him.

"You are going to America, to that dude ranch. You will find out," he was told. "And if Luca Rossi is alive, you will make sure he dies."

He shuddered then at the thought of pulling the trigger himself, of ending Luca's life.

"It's him or you…"

And that was why he had no choice. He had to do what they wanted. He had to live, even though that meant Luca had to die.

Chapter 12

The break in the storm that Jasper had mentioned came with daybreak. Kayla had made it to the barn. Fortunately Aubrey and Luke were dressed by then and in the stall with the calf. Or she might have known for certain what she probably only suspected.

For she'd cast them a strange glance when she found them in the stall, crouching close together over the calf. Or maybe Aubrey was just paranoid that everyone else could see how much she was affected from her night with Luke.

She was worried most of all that he would see it, that he would see how much she wanted from him. And she knew the thing she wanted most, he couldn't give her: honesty.

So none of the rest of it mattered.

"Jasper said you made it back last night," Kayla said.

"And I saw, as I drove here, that the rest of the cattle were in the pasture by the indoor ring. But who's this little guy?"

"An orphan," Aubrey replied. "Luke carried him all the way back."

Kayla looked at him then and nodded. "That's not the easiest thing to do when it isn't a blizzard. These calves weigh more than you think."

Luke was strong. Aubrey knew that because he'd lifted her a few times last night as if she hadn't weighed much more than the calf.

Luke gently patted the animal's head. "He was worth it."

That was how Aubrey had decided to look at last night. That all the pleasure he'd given her would be worth the pain that would surely follow when he left. And as if he was eager to leave now, he asked Kayla, "How are the roads?"

"Jasper has the grounds crew clearing the roads on the ranch," she said. "I'm not sure about the main streets. Why are you asking? Are you leaving?"

He hesitated just long enough for Aubrey to know that he was. And a pang struck her heart so sharply that she nearly gasped.

"I was just curious," he replied.

Just curious if he could leave or if he was trapped here with her?

Aubrey didn't ask.

"I doubt the street coming out here from Blue Larkspur is clear yet," Kayla said. "The road crews will focus on the city first."

He nodded. "Of course."

"Jasper does want you to head up to the main lodge right away," Kayla told Aubrey. "He's anxious to talk to you."

"He could have called me," Aubrey said. "I know cell reception isn't the best right now, but there's the landline in the tack room."

Kayla shrugged. "He must have tried—said you weren't picking up."

Had the phone rung? Aubrey had been so preoccupied with Luke that she might not have noticed. Heat flushed her face, and she looked away from Kayla, who was studying her a little intently.

Was she judging Aubrey for crossing a line with a guest? Maybe that was why Jasper was so anxious to talk to her—to remind her that Luke was a guest. And she was one of the owners, responsible for the ranch and everyone on it.

And with the blizzard hitting, there was probably a lot to attend to—which Jasper had been doing on his own. Now she felt a pang of guilt.

"Can you call the vet and see if she can make it out here on her snowmobile or at least advise you on how to check out the calf?" Aubrey asked her.

Kayla nodded.

"Then I better get up to the main lodge and see what Jasper needs," Aubrey said and she stepped out of the stall.

Luke followed her out. "I'll go with you."

She waited until they were walking out the side barn door to her snow-covered truck before she asked, "Why?"

"You probably have a lot you need to do with the storm hitting," he said. "I can help."

"You've already done so much…" And not just in moving the cattle.

Even now he was using his arm to knock the snow from the hood of her truck.

She unlocked the door and reached inside for the snow brush. Then she started the engine to warm it up. Not that she was cold…

Just being close to Luke had her body heating up, as thoughts of the night before, of all the places he'd touched her, kissed her, played through her mind. He had already done so much.

He'd made her feel beautiful and desirable in a way nobody else ever had. But she couldn't allow herself to get used to being with him, especially like they'd been last night or even like the past couple of days that they'd moved the cattle, working together—instinctively anticipating what the other needed. Just like when they'd made love…

She couldn't remember ever having a connection like that with another human being. And feeling overwhelmed by it, she offered, "I can drop you at your cabin."

He shook his head. "I don't think I have any food left. I'd like to check out the dining room at the main lodge. For some reason I'm starving." He patted his flat stomach, and she remembered what he looked like beneath the heavy coat and his shirt, how his washboard abs had rippled when he moved, when she…

Her breath caught at the image, at the memory, at

the burning desire to do it again, to make love with him over and over.

He must have noticed her reaction because his eyes dilated until the blue of his irises was just a thin circle around the black. "Or maybe we should go back to my cabin. Or your house…"

She wanted to—so badly, but she forced herself to shake her head. "I better talk to Jasper before he sends out a search party."

"I'm kind of surprised he didn't do that last night," Luke said.

"He trusts that I can take care of myself," Aubrey said with pride.

"He knows you well," Luke remarked.

"It's the twin intuition thing," she said. But even that didn't compare to her connection with Luke.

Luke had cleared the snow from the truck, and now hopped into the passenger seat. She could have tried to drop him at his cabin, but she had a feeling he might not get out of the pickup. So she drove him up to the main lodge like he wanted.

But when they walked into the great room together, Aubrey felt as if everyone turned and stared at them. She probably looked a mess since she hadn't showered or changed her clothes. She probably had straw in her hair and scrapes on her skin from Luke's stubble—dead giveaways to how they'd spent the night. So she felt as if she was doing the walk of shame with everyone watching her and judging her.

Which made no sense. She was probably just paranoid because she knew what she'd done wasn't smart—

for so many reasons. She'd broken her own rule of never getting involved with another man she couldn't trust.

Now Luca remembered why he hadn't come up to the main lodge before. There were too many people. Too many people who could be hurt if someone tried to take him out here like they had at that B and B in Toronto and that hotel in Wisconsin.

Unless those had just been strange coincidences. But he doubted that, just as he doubted those gunshots had been for a mountain lion or a coyote. They'd been meant for him.

And if someone tried again to take him out on the ranch, there were more people who could be hurt. More people than just Aubrey—although her being in harm's way would affect him the most.

In the enormous great room, there were a few families with kids, some couples, and they were all staring at him and Aubrey now. Maybe they were just curious about him because he hadn't come up to the main lodge before, and he was a stranger to them. A stranger who'd showed up during a storm when the roads were supposedly impassable...

Despite the grounds crew working on the roads on the ranch, they had still been snow-covered and slippery. But just as she was good at everything else, Aubrey was a skilled driver.

There were some things that she was better than good at, things at which she excelled, like making love. He'd never had a more responsive, more generous partner than Aubrey Colton. And he suspected that he never would.

Leaving this place, leaving her, was going to be the hardest thing he'd ever had to do. Maybe harder even than leaving his country and his family.

And yet they barely knew each other. Hell, she didn't even know his real name. Because of that, because of the lies he'd had to tell her, they had no future.

Luca suspected that if he didn't get off the ranch soon, he would have no future on his own, either. Because it didn't feel like everyone was watching them with just mild curiosity.

Someone was staring at him intently, almost malevolently—Aubrey's twin. Jasper asked, "Where the hell have you been?" He might have been addressing Aubrey, but he was staring at Luca.

"What?" Luca asked in confusion. "You were expecting me?"

"No," Jasper said. "I wasn't." He turned toward his sister. "I was trying to call you back last night in the barn, but you didn't pick up."

"I was fine," she said.

Jasper stared intently at her for a long moment before glancing back at Luca. "Dominic called me to check on you."

Was he still talking to her? Or to Luca?

Aubrey must have been confused as well, because she asked, "Check on me?"

Jasper narrowed his eyes and gave her a pointed stare, as if he was silently communicating with her.

Aubrey must not have picked up on his silent message because she shrugged off his concern. "He had no reason to check up on me. I'm fine."

Apparently the FBI agent had found just enough to

raise his suspicions and apparently Jasper's even more. Was Jasper the one who'd searched Luca's cabin? And had it been on his other brother's orders or because of his own suspicions?

"He has concerns," Jasper said. "Especially when I told him about those gunshots."

"And I told you that those gunshots were probably from another rancher who was firing at a wild animal."

"I talked to the other guests who heard the shots," Jasper said. "It sounds like they came from the direction of the Sutherlands'."

Some of the tightness in Luca's chest eased; that was good, then. Another rancher had fired those shots just like Aubrey had thought.

But she was tense now and her face pale. "How could anyone even be staying out there since the fire?" she asked.

Jasper shrugged. "Mr. Sutherland sure isn't. Nadine isn't going to let her dad come back out until the place is rebuilt. So who would have fired those shots, Aubrey?"

She shook her head. "I don't know. Caleb is getting a contract ready for us to sign a lease on the pastures. There hasn't been any livestock out there in years. So what would anyone be doing on that property?"

Jasper's brow furrowed. "Could it have anything to do with that oil company that was trying to take Al Sutherland's fracking rights before Caleb and Nadine stopped them?"

Luca narrowed his eyes at the other man's tone. "There were issues with this company?"

Jasper nodded. "There were some dangerous people working for it."

"Maybe somebody from that place came back," Aubrey suggested.

"Where is the Sutherland property?" Luca asked. "I can ride over and check it out." If someone pointed him in the right direction...

"The roads are impassable outside the ranch," Jasper said.

Luca nodded. "But surely a horse could get through."

"With the snow and drifting it wouldn't be safe on horseback," Jasper said. "The snowmobiles would be an easier and faster way to get there."

"I need to check out the ranch," Luca said. Even though he'd never ridden a snowmobile, he was determined to find out what those gunshots had really been about, if someone had found him...or if it was safe—especially with Aubrey in mind—for him to stay awhile longer.

"Why?" Jasper asked him. "What's your interest in all this?"

Aubrey's twin was definitely suspicious of Luca, and rightfully so.

"Those gunshots seemed like they were close to us," Luca admitted. Much too close. "I just want to make sure that it wasn't personal."

"Why would it be personal?" Jasper persisted.

Luca shrugged. "I wasn't the only one in that area where the shots were fired," he pointed out. And he glanced at Aubrey.

"I was the one who pushed for us to lease the Sutherland property," she said. "Maybe the oil company is trying to scare us away from it."

Jasper shook his head. "Caleb got the company's

henchmen to turn on the executives. If they were going to go after anyone, it would probably be him. I can't imagine who would want to hurt you, Aubrey."

Neither could Luca but then he remembered the ugly encounter she'd had in her driveway. "Warren Parker wasn't happy the other night with the way she got rid of him."

"Warren…" Aubrey gasped. "I forgot all about him…"

Luca's heart swelled with relief. He was ridiculously happy that she'd forgotten all about her ex-boyfriend. Unfortunately, so had Luca. Was it possible that Warren Parker had been trying to eliminate his competition for Aubrey's heart? No. Warren didn't want her heart; he wanted her money. He was a desperate man, and Luca shouldn't have forgotten that.

If it was Warren who'd tried for him, he was safe. He could stay, but even then, he wasn't sure that he should—because then he would definitely fall for Aubrey Colton if he hadn't already.

"Come with me, then," Luca said to Jasper. "Let's check out the Sutherland property and see if anyone is staying there."

"I'm going, too," Aubrey said.

"Neither one of you needs to go," Jasper said—to them both. "I can take a fast ride out there and see if it's as deserted as I think it is."

Luca shook his head. "No. The weather is still bad. Nobody should go alone." If Warren Parker was willing to shoot at them, he might go after Jasper, too.

And if it hadn't been Warren or someone from that oil company…

Then he'd been right, and somehow the Camorra had figured out where he was, and they had no problem with collateral damage in their quest for revenge against him. They could have killed other guests at the hotel or B and B fires. Luca didn't want anyone else to become collateral damage in the hit on his life.

Luca Rossi. Sure, he was calling himself Luke Bishop now, but the assassin recognized him from the picture he'd been given with the envelope of cash. The cash had been enough to pay for two killers, but he'd already cut his partner out of this deal before they'd left for the ranch.

He hadn't wanted to share that money. The initial down payment, or the payoff he would receive when they had proof that Luca Rossi was dead. And he needed the proof—not just to receive the payout but so that he himself wasn't eliminated.

Like those other guys had been by the Camorra for their failures.

His predecessors had failed to take out Luca Rossi in any of those other cities where they'd been tipped off he was staying. The target wasn't a master spy; he was just a journalist.

Rossi should have been easy to kill.

He should have died yesterday. But the guy didn't have a scratch on him. How the hell had he missed? Had he been too far away?

The next time he would have to make sure he was very close, so that Rossi didn't escape death yet again. And, from eavesdropping on the conversation Rossi had

had with the owners of the dude ranch, he knew where Luca was going to be. And he intended to be there, too.

If the Coltons got in his way, then Luca Rossi wouldn't be the only one dying today.

Chapter 13

Warren...

Why hadn't Aubrey considered that he might have had something to do with those gunshots? Probably because she didn't want to admit she'd once dated such a loser. It was bad enough that he'd lied and manipulated her. But to have fired those shots...

Then she remembered the yellowed bruise around his eyes. Maybe he was so desperate to pay off his debts that he'd become dangerous.

Aubrey shivered and it had nothing to do with the cold. She wore a heavy snowmobile suit, gloves and a helmet. So, despite the cold air rushing over her as she sped along, she felt warm. Probably because Luke was pressed against her back, his arms wrapped around her waist.

While he had experience riding horses, he'd admitted to never driving a snowmobile before. She'd tried to get him to remain behind at the ranch and not just because she didn't have the time to give him the lessons that they gave their other guests before they allowed them to use the snowmobiles. She hadn't wanted Luke riding along with her and Jasper. She'd wanted to talk to her twin alone and find out what was wrong exactly.

What had Dominic said to him? Because it was clear that he didn't trust Luke now. In her head, she knew that she shouldn't, either, but in her heart...

She just couldn't believe that he was a bad man. But maybe that was because she was already falling for him.

Why had Luke been so intent on checking out those gunshots? Because of the dangerous people he'd admitted to meeting in his research? Were those people after him now?

He must have thought so, or he wouldn't have been so concerned. He'd tried talking her out of going to the Sutherlands', like he wanted to protect her, like he didn't want to put her in harm's way.

But if Warren was the one who'd fired those shots, then she was the one who'd put Luke in peril.

And if the blizzard had forced Warren to hole up on the Sutherland property, then Jasper could be in danger now as well. But her twin had also been insistent on going along, almost as if he didn't trust her to be alone with Luke.

Maybe it was twin intuition, and he somehow knew that even she didn't trust herself to be alone with Luke. Not because of what he would do but because of what she would do—fall so completely for him that she would get her heart broken for certain. Maybe it was already too late for that.

Jasper had stared most intently at them when they'd entered the great room earlier, like he'd been trying to figure out what was going on between them. He wasn't the only one…

But she'd known what she was doing last night, known that last night might be the only chance she had to be with Luke, to find out if the attraction between them was as powerful as she'd suspected.

It had been more…

So much more.

But that one night would have to be enough—just as she'd determined it was going to be the night before. Maybe, so that she didn't risk falling for him, she would have even been more comfortable if she'd dropped Luke off at his cabin and had never seen him again.

Not that she could see him now but she could feel him. Even through their heavy snowsuits, she could feel the heat and hardness of his body. She wanted to lean into him, but somehow, even with his helmet on, she knew that Jasper was watching them, wondering…

And Aubrey suddenly wondered if he was the only one watching them. Despite the warmth of Luke's body, a sudden chill rushed over her. It wasn't the wind; that had subsided during this break in the storm. The sun was shining, glistening off the snow-covered ground. No. The weather was calm; the storm was inside Aubrey, making her uneasy.

Maybe it was because they were fast approaching the Sutherland property. What if Warren was here? If he was the one who'd fired the shots the day before, then he was armed.

They slowed as they neared the Sutherlands' barn. It was one of just a few structures standing yet on the property. The house had burned, but now even the charred remains of it were gone. People had been working on rebuilding, and maybe someone still was, because despite the storm, another snowmobile was already parked near the barn.

Luke leaned close to her, his helmet bumping against hers, and he advised her, "Kill the engine." Then with a chopping signal with his gloved hand, he gestured for Jasper to do the same.

If it was Warren's snowmobile—and Aubrey knew he had one unless he'd sold it to pay off some of his mounting debts—then he would have already heard them driving up. There wasn't any escaping now... unless they turned around and fled.

But Luke seemed determined to face the danger head-on; he jumped off and rushed toward the barn, pulling his helmet off as he ran. Jasper pulled off his helmet, dropped it onto the seat of his snowmobile, and followed closely behind Luke. Aubrey then tried to catch them, but their legs were longer and the snow was so deep. When she started toward the barn, she sank into a drift up to her thighs.

If that was Warren's snowmobile, if he was holed up in the barn with that weapon, and he hurt either of them...

She would never forgive herself for bringing that man into their lives. "Wait!" she called out to them. "Remember, he has a gun."

"How do you know?" a deep voice asked, and a man stepped out of the open door of the barn. He held a long gun in his gloved hand, but his fingers were nowhere near the trigger. "And do any of you know what the hell this gun was doing here?"

Luke stopped in front of her, turning toward her as if trying to shield her with his body. As if he expected this man to shoot her.

She smiled reassuringly at him and said, "This is my oldest brother, Caleb. His fiancée, Nadine Sutherland, owns the property—but we're going to lease it for grazing."

Nadine stepped out of the barn behind Caleb. Like the rest of them, she was bundled up in a snowmobile suit, the hood covering most of her shoulder-length brown hair but for a few auburn-kissed strands that had slipped out to frame her beautiful face.

"And this is Nadine," she said.

"What are you guys doing out here?" Jasper asked. "How did you even get out of town?"

Caleb pointed to the snowmobile. "Same way you did," he said.

"But you don't own one," Jasper said.

"I borrowed one from a client," Caleb replied. "Nadine got a call yesterday that there was someone shooting around here, and we wanted to check the place out. Make sure nobody from Rutledge Oil was causing trouble again. And we found this…" He held up the gun. Then he focused his lawyerly gaze on Luke like he was on the witness stand. "Who's this?"

Aubrey wasn't sure how to introduce Luke. He was

more than a guest but less than a boyfriend. A one-night stand?

Luke saved her the trouble when he stepped forward to extend his hand to Caleb. "Luke Bishop. I'm staying at the Gemini Ranch."

Caleb shook Luke's hand, but his brow furrowed beneath the fall of brown hair that stuck out beneath his hat. He glanced from Luke to Aubrey and back. "A guest?"

"He's been helping out during the storm," Aubrey explained.

"We heard those shots yesterday while we were moving the cattle. They sounded like they came close to us," Luke explained, "so we wanted to check it out."

Caleb was checking him out now, his eyes narrowed in speculation.

"When you were driving up on your snowmobile, did you see anyone around here?" Luke asked.

Caleb shook his head.

"Does anyone come around to check on the place besides you? A caretaker?" Luke asked, and now *he* sounded like a lawyer. Or an investigator…

Caleb shook his head again. "No. Do you have any ideas about why someone might have been shooting at you?"

"I don't think they were shooting at us," Aubrey said. At least she hoped not. "You know how sounds echo around the mountains."

Jasper pointed at the gun. "Well, the other guests were right when they indicated the sound of shots came from this direction. Any idea who might have been out here?" he asked Nadine.

She shook her head. "I don't know. Maybe one of the other neighbors. They feel bad that they didn't know what was going on with my dad…"

Al Sutherland was in the early stages of dementia, but he was so proud he hadn't admitted to anyone that he was having trouble remembering things. And that oil company had taken advantage of his age and his pride until Nadine had gotten Caleb involved.

"One of the neighbors called me about the gunshots they heard," Nadine continued, "asking if I was letting anyone hunt on the property."

"Have you given anyone permission?" Luke asked.

Nadine shook her head again. "I haven't, but my father probably has. I will ask him, but I doubt he'll remember who he told…"

Caleb slid his free arm around Nadine's shoulders, pulling her close to his side to comfort her. Al Sutherland had been a difficult man without the dementia. So very proud. Too proud to ask for help when he'd needed it.

If not for Nadine and Caleb's intervention, Rutledge Oil would have gotten away with their horrible plans.

Aubrey gazed around the beautiful property and shuddered over what it might have become. She was thrilled Gemini Ranch would be leasing the pastures for their own livestock.

"Maybe that's all it was, then," Jasper said. "Somebody hunting…"

Her twin didn't sound any more convinced of that than Aubrey was now, since Luke had mentioned Warren. Her ex-boyfriend had been unusually persistent lately with the texts and the calls and then showing up as he had at her house. No, not just persistent. He was clearly desperate.

"Why would a hunter leave their gun behind?" Aubrey asked.

Caleb shrugged. "Maybe they intend to come back."

"Do you mind if I look around?" Luke asked.

Caleb shrugged. "Suit yourself…"

Nadine gestured toward Aubrey. "Come in here and see our plans for the house. We've tacked them up on the barn wall."

Aubrey glanced at Luke, who was walking around the area near the barn, as if looking for tracks. But after last night's storm, she doubted he would be able to find anything that would lead to the location of the shooter. And since Caleb had the gun, she wasn't worried about him getting shot at again, so she followed Nadine inside.

"What's with your guest?" Caleb asked Jasper, as her twin passed their oldest brother.

"Ask Aubrey," Jasper said. "Or better yet, Dominic."

"Dominic?" Caleb asked, his voice sharp with concern. "What's going on?"

Aubrey shook her head. "Nothing." Then she glared at Jasper. "Just my brothers overreacting. That's all that's going on—the usual."

Nadine chuckled and linked her arm through Aubrey's, tugging her farther inside the barn. "He's good-looking," she remarked.

Clearly she'd picked up on Aubrey's attraction to their guest. Unable to deny the truth, she just nodded and agreed, "Yes, he is…"

And Nadine hadn't even seen him without those clothes.

The image of Luke's long, leanly muscled body flashed through Aubrey's mind and heat flashed through her body, despite the coldness of the empty building.

Nadine chuckled again and pulled Aubrey over to the wall where the construction plans hung. "We're going to completely rebuild the house. It's going to have a private wing for my dad," Nadine said, pointing to the print. "And a lot of bedrooms for all the kids we want to have…"

Caleb and Jasper had joined them, and Caleb slid his arm around his fiancée again. Pulling her back against his body, he kissed the side of her face. "It's going to be perfect," Caleb agreed. "Just like you…"

Aubrey's heart swelled with love and happiness for them, but a pang of envy struck her as well. She wanted that for herself. She wanted what they had.

But would she ever find it when she kept falling only for men she couldn't trust?

Maybe they intend to come back…

Caleb Colton's words echoed in Luca's head. That was his fear. That whoever had left that weapon behind planned to return for it. To use it again if they'd not been successful the first time.

Had that person been Warren Parker—intent on eliminating the competition? Or had it been someone carrying out the Camorra's hit on Luca Rossi?

Too much snow had fallen to see any tracks beyond the ones from Caleb and Nadine's snowmobile and Aubrey's and Jasper's. But someone had been out here, someone had left the gun in the barn.

Luca stepped inside, where everyone had gathered

around the plans hanging on one of the barn walls. The four of them laughed and teased each other, and there was so much love that longing struck Luca's heart. And he saw that emotion on Aubrey's face as well.

She wanted this—the kind of future her oldest brother was planning with his fiancée. The house. The kids...

Luca had never considered that kind of future for himself. Had never imagined himself a husband or a father.

He'd always seen himself chasing the next story. But now that last story kept chasing him, trying to kill him. And if he died, what would he leave behind? Who would mourn him besides his mother and some relatives?

And he wondered now about some of those relatives...

At least one.

Or had he been wrong to suspect his cousin of betraying him? Maybe it was that idiot Warren Parker who'd fired those shots. He really hoped it was, even though he could tell that the thought upset Aubrey, undermining her self-confidence even more than Warren's manipulative, backhanded remarks already had.

Aubrey doubted her desirability because of Warren. But she also doubted her own judgment because of Warren and because of Luca. His heart ached that he couldn't be honest with her, that he couldn't tell her everything.

While everyone else studied those plans, he studied her face, watching every emotion play across it. She was so expressive, so genuine...

She deserved someone who could be as sincere as she was. She deserved someone better than a man with a price on his head.

He dragged his gaze away from her and found that someone was watching him. Nadine. The woman studied his face like he'd been studying Aubrey's. What had she seen?

A small smile curved her lips as if she knew or had realized something that no one else knew. Even Luca?

A shiver chased down his spine. The wind returned, a gust of it pushing open the door Luca had closed behind himself. The cold breeze rattled the papers on the wall.

"Oh no," Aubrey said. "Do you want to take them down?"

"We have more than one copy," Caleb said.

He seemed like the kind of guy who would be thorough, who would make sure all the bases were covered. Every one of Aubrey's siblings that Luca had met had impressed him. But what impressed him most was how much they seemed to love each other.

"We should head back to the lodge," Jasper said. "I don't think this break is going to last much longer before the snow starts up again. Why don't you two come back with us?"

"Yes," Aubrey said. "We need to talk about your wedding. Summer will be here before we know it. We want to make sure we have everything ready at the ranch for it."

Nadine shivered inside her snowsuit. "Doesn't feel like summer is coming, and it can't get here fast enough for me."

"Or me," Caleb agreed. "But we'll have to talk wedding plans another time. I have too much to do in town, with work and the Truth Foundation."

"Have you found out anything about Ronald Spence's claims of innocence?" Aubrey asked, and she sounded suspicious.

"Not yet," Caleb said. "But Rebekah is busy working on it."

"Rebekah is Caleb and Morgan's brilliant assistant," Nadine informed Luca. "If there's evidence to be found, she'll find it."

Too bad Rebekah hadn't come out to the ranch with them; maybe she would have found a clue Luca had missed. Because he had no way of knowing for certain who'd fired those shots or why.

They all left the barn together, walking out to their snowmobiles. Caleb held on to the gun he'd found.

"What are you going to do with that?" Luca wondered.

Caleb glanced at it like he'd forgotten that he had it. "It might belong to one of my future father-in-law's friends, so I'm going to hang on to it. See if anyone claims it."

Luca nodded because he couldn't argue with the man. And it wasn't as if he had any connections in Blue Larkspur like he'd had in Naples. He couldn't ask someone to check the registration on it or run a ballistics test.

"Turn it over to Chief Lawson," Jasper recommended. "He should be able to find out who it belongs to. We should know who was firing that thing up here and why." He was staring at Luca now, and his interest drew the oldest brother's gaze to him, too.

Their scrutiny unsettled him, but he suspected they weren't the only ones staring at him. When he glanced at Nadine, though, she wasn't studying him like she had earlier, in the barn. She was engaged in a quiet conversation with Aubrey.

But beyond them, in the fringe of trees around what must have been the foundation of the burned-down farmhouse, Luca noticed something. Between some of those fire-blackened branches, he caught a movement of some sort, a shadow…

Was somebody out there, watching him or all of them?

Caleb stared after the snowmobiles as they headed away from the Sutherlands'—from his future home— toward Gemini Ranch. Luke Bishop had his arms wrapped around his sister, and Caleb didn't much care for it. And it wasn't just because Aubrey was his younger sibling. A man she shouldn't have trusted had already hurt her, and Caleb was worried that it was about to happen again.

"What do you think about Luke Bishop?" he asked his fiancée. Nadine was a good judge of character.

She smiled. "I think that he's at least halfway in love with your sister, if not all the way," she said.

And Caleb groaned.

"She's not just your little sister," Nadine said, and now her smile was a teasing one. "She's also a beautiful woman."

"I know that," Caleb said.

"Do you know that she's also smart and strong and can take care of herself?"

Caleb narrowed his eyes as if glaring at her even as a grin tugged up his lips. "Yes. But I worry about her. That last guy she dated was a loser."

"And from what I've heard about that situation, Aubrey figured out quickly what the creep was really after, and she didn't fall for him," Nadine said. Her smile slipped away then. "But it might already be too late for her now. Not that I think Luke Bishop is a creep…"

But clearly, she didn't know quite what to make of the man, either.

"When we get back to town, I'm going to call Dominic," Caleb said. "See what he knows about Luke Bishop."

Nadine cocked her head. "Hear that?" she asked.

"What?" he asked. All he could hear was the sound of the snowmobile engines echoing around them. Sounds did carry out here.

"I thought I heard a third snowmobile starting up," Nadine replied.

Caleb's pulse quickened. "You think someone else is hanging around here." He gripped the gun more tightly in his hand. "Coming back for this…"

And when he'd seen them, instead of walking up to talk to them, he'd taken off so he wouldn't be seen. Caleb released a shaky sigh. He'd thought it was all over; that no more bad things were going to happen at Nadine's father's ranch.

"It's going to be fine," his fiancée said, as if she'd

read his mind. "We're going to build our beautiful home here and start our family."

She was right. They were going to be fine. It was his siblings whom Caleb was worried about now. Specifically Aubrey…

Chapter 14

Luke's arms tightened around Aubrey, and he leaned over her, his helmet bumping against hers. "There's another snowmobile behind us," he yelled. "And it's not Jasper."

Her pulse quickened, but that was from his closeness, from his breath against her neck. She wasn't worried about the other snowmobiler.

"Caleb and Nadine probably changed their minds," she shouted back at him. She hadn't been exaggerating when she said that summer would be here before they knew it. It was already March, and there was a lot of planning to do for the wedding yet.

Next to her, Jasper turned and glanced over his shoulder. He'd seen it, too.

They weren't far from the ranch now. The sled was the same color as theirs, and as close as it was drawing to them, it was possible that there might have been the Gemini Ranch symbol on the hood of it. If it was one of their sleds, then it was probably a guest out for a solo ride. Or one of the staff coming to get her and Jasper. Maybe the generators had stopped working or there was an issue with the livestock. The calf...

Jasper must have been having the same thoughts and concerns because he stopped his snowmobile just as she stopped hers.

"What are you doing?" Luke asked, his voice gruff with concern. "You should keep driving. Wait until we get back to the ranch."

"It might be Kayla or one of the other hands," Jasper said.

Interesting that his first thought was of Kayla. Aubrey had begun to wonder about her brother's interest in her. Not that he ever acted interested in her or she in him whenever they were together.

It was almost as if they made an effort to ignore each other. She doubted it was Kayla. For one, the rider was obviously bigger than Kayla. Bigger than Aubrey, too.

This wasn't a woman driving the other snowmobile. But the rider's helmet had a tinted mask on it, hiding their face. Before Aubrey could take another look at the rider, Luke jumped off the back of her sled and stepped between her and the other snowmobile. She tensed, waiting for it to pass them, but it drew to a stop, the driver's gloved hand on the brake. The engine still ran, as if the driver wanted to make a quick escape.

Jasper jumped off his sled, too, and gestured for the person to kill his engine. But the rider revved it instead before finally lifting the shield on his helmet.

Leaning around Luke, she could see the man's face, and anger had her heart slamming against her ribs. She jumped off the sled. "Warren! What the hell are you doing out here?"

She'd tossed him off the ranch two nights ago.

"I want to talk to you," he said, his tone petulant.

"So you stole one of our snowmobiles?" Jasper asked.

Heat flushed Aubrey's face with embarrassment that she'd shown Warren where everything was on the ranch. Apparently she'd shown him too much.

"I'm just borrowing it," Warren said. Probably because he'd sold his, just as she'd wondered if he'd had to, to pay off his debts.

"How'd you get out here from town?" Luke asked. "The roads are impassable."

"Not that it's any of your damn business but I didn't stay in town," he said. He turned back to Aubrey now, his face flushed with his own anger. "Where were you last night?"

She gasped. "You were at my house? How did you get inside?"

"He must've broken in," Luke answered for him, "after he shot at us."

"Shot at you!" Warren exclaimed. "What the hell are you talking about?"

"You know," Luke insisted.

"I'm going to call the police chief," Jasper said. But when he pulled out his cell phone, he grimaced slightly. And Aubrey knew that his phone must be dead or at least without service. Hers had to be the same; she hadn't charged it last night.

And Luke…

His cell phones were in his trash. But he wasn't reaching for his phone, he was reaching for Warren. Before he could pull the other man from the snowmobile, though, Warren released the brake and headed toward him. One of the skis struck Luke, knocking him back. Since he'd been so intent on staying between her and Warren, he fell into her.

She grabbed at him, trying to hold him up. But he jerked away and started after Warren. Her ex-boyfriend revved the engine and took off, sending a spray of snow back at them—into their faces.

Jasper sputtered, too, then jumped back on his sled. "Don't!" she yelled before he could start it. "Don't chase him! Just let him go."

Luke turned toward her now. "Let him go?"

"He's dangerous," she said. "If he was the one who fired those shots yesterday—"

"Then he left his gun behind," Jasper interrupted her.

"He might have another," Luke admitted. "And if he broke into her place and took the snowmobile, you need to call the police chief like you said you were going to."

Shame rushed over Aubrey, churning in her stomach. For some reason she didn't want the chief—didn't want anyone else—to know how stupid she'd been to get involved with a man like Warren Parker.

"Wait," she said.

"You don't want to call the police on him?" Jasper asked.

"Call Caleb," she said. "Make sure he brings that gun to the chief. If it's Warren's or can be traced to him, then yes, we need to call the police. But right now we don't know that it's his weapon. We don't know that he broke into my place or the snowmobile shed." He could have paid attention when she'd entered the code for the door lock—which was an electronic one like the ones on all the cabins and rooms in the lodge. He could have remembered how to get inside.

But if he knew the code, he could claim that she'd given it to him. And all of this would just be a messy case of "he said, she said," with no proof to support their suspicions about Warren Parker.

"He stole that snowmobile. Even if you don't believe he fired those shots yesterday, he should be arrested for theft."

Jasper nodded in agreement. "He will be. I'm going back to the lodge. I'm going to call the police."

Aubrey figured the chief would come out—even though it wasn't a big theft. He seemed to have some kind of personal interest in their family—maybe because of what their father had done. Or maybe because of their mother...

Isa Colton was a beautiful woman; Aubrey had been told that she looked like her. Sometimes when she looked at older photos of Isa she could see it, and she certainly hoped she aged as well as her mother had. Mama was a beautiful seventy-two with her blond hair cut to shoulder length and a full figure that still made men turn their heads when she entered a room. Along with her looks, she had talent—as an artist. She also had a strength that Aubrey envied—the strength to survive her husband's betrayal and raise twelve kids on her own.

Mama had been fooled, so maybe Aubrey shouldn't feel so bad about Warren having momentarily fooled her. Unlike Aubrey her mother had made certain to never trust another man. Not that Aubrey trusted Luke...

But she hadn't been able to resist her attraction to him, either.

She continued to resist his and her brother's insistence on calling the police, though. "It's going to be a waste of time investigating a snowmobile theft." For an officer and especially for the chief. "I'm sure it will soon be found somewhere on the property."

And when Warren was questioned, he would swear that she'd told him he could use them anytime. And nearly a year ago, she probably had—before she'd learned about his gambling and that getting her to pay off his debts was his real reason for dating her.

"He's dangerous," Jasper said. "You need to come back to the lodge with me."

Aubrey shook her head. "I can handle Warren," she insisted. She wasn't sure she could handle the humiliation of being involved with a loser like him, though.

She could barely look at Luke. If Warren had fired those shots, and it certainly looked like he had, then Luke could have been killed because of her. Because of the mistakes she'd made...

Luca wasn't sure what was going on, why Aubrey didn't want her brother calling the police. But Jasper had insisted on doing it and had ridden off on his snowmobile toward the main lodge.

"You should have gone with him," she said.

He shook his head. "I'm not leaving you alone. Jasper's right. You should go back there, too."

"I'm going to check on my house," she said.

He'd known she was going to stubbornly insist on it; that was another reason he hadn't gone with Jasper—though the man had offered. Warren Parker showing up when he had, on a stolen snowmobile, must have allayed whatever suspicions Jasper had had about Luca.

About Luke Bishop…

A pang of regret struck Luca that he had to lie to all of them. But most especially to Aubrey.

She deserved better, especially after being involved with a guy like Warren Parker.

"I'm going with you," Luca insisted, but as he started toward the snowmobile, pain shot up his leg, and he stumbled and nearly fell.

"Oh my God, are you all right?" she asked.

He glanced down at the snowmobile suit he wore—the material on one of the legs was torn.

"You're bleeding," she said.

If he was, it was too cold for him to feel it; and now that his suit was torn, he could feel the cold. The wind was beginning to whip up again—just a gust here and there, not yet the sustained fury of the night before.

And only a few random snowflakes drifted down from the dark clouds hanging overhead. It seemed as if the storm was hovering just out of reach for now, but it wasn't done with them yet.

Kind of like the Camorra…

Even if they hadn't found Luca yet, they would. And they certainly weren't done with him yet. They wouldn't be until he was dead.

Just as Warren didn't seem done with Aubrey yet. What was he going to do to her, though? How did he think he was going to change her mind about giving him money?

"I'm fine," Luca insisted, and he managed to suppress the grimace of pain that threatened to cross his face when he hobbled the couple of feet through the deep snow to the machine.

Aubrey had already jumped on it, and he swung his leg over the seat and climbed onto it. "I'm taking you back to the lodge," she said as she turned back toward him. The face shield was up on her helmet, so that he could see the furrows on her brow, the concern for him. "And maybe the roads will be clear enough to get you to town."

"I'm fine," he insisted. "It's not broken." Or he would have fallen on his face. "It's just a scrape. Let's get back to your house and make sure that it's secure."

"But if Warren's there…"

"You'll protect me," he said with a smile.

She didn't smile back, and her blue eyes darkened more with concern. "I'm sorry," she murmured.

"For what?" he asked.

"That you were hurt—"

"I'm fine," he insisted.

"You could have been hurt worse," she said. "With the snowmobile and with those gunshots. If that is Warren's gun, he probably was firing at you, trying to get you out of his way."

"We don't know that it is Warren's gun," he reminded her. And he had a niggling doubt that it wasn't, that Luca was instead the one who'd put her in danger.

But he didn't know for certain…

It could have been Warren. The man was certainly acting desperate enough that he might have shot at him.

"Let's go to your house," he said. "Let's check it out."

She nodded in agreement. "And we can look at your leg. See how bad it is, if you'll need stitches…"

He grimaced now.

"Not a fan of hospitals?"

He shook his head. But it wasn't just his injury that concerned him. He had that sensation again, that feeling he'd had earlier when he'd noticed someone around the Sutherland barn. Someone was still watching them.

At last they were alone…

Just Rossi and that woman, Aubrey Colton. Earlier there had been the other man, Jasper Colton, and then the other one.

The one who'd been skulking around the ranch, sticking close to them but not close enough that he would have been able to kill them all. Somebody could have served as a witness to the assassination.

He *would* leave no witnesses behind to identify him. He waited a few moments until he started up his snowmobile again, wanting to make sure that anyone else was far enough away that they wouldn't hear it.

It didn't matter, though. He'd heard them. He knew where they were going, back to her house, which was perfect. It was near Rossi's little cabin, and far enough away from the rest of the ranch that nobody would see or hear the murders.

Because now he had no choice. With the woman sticking as close as she was to Luca Rossi, she had sealed her fate.

Or Luca had sealed it for her.

She was going to die. Just as—*finally*—Luca Rossi was going to die.

Chapter 15

Aubrey knew someone had been in her home the moment she opened the door, and a shudder of revulsion rippled down her spine. Luke must have noticed, too, because he caught her arm and held her back from stepping over the threshold.

"Wait," he said. "He could still be in here."

She shook her head. "No. We didn't see any fresh tracks." But there had definitely been tracks from another snowmobile outside and footprints from someone walking out of the French doors and across the deck that spanned the front of it. She shuddered again at the invasion of her privacy, of her space, and suddenly she realized how Luke must have felt when he'd found her in his cabin.

"I'm sorry," she said, guilt weighing so heavily on her for that and for his getting injured. "Let's get you inside and take a look at that leg."

She would deal with Warren later, or better yet, she would let the police deal with him. Jasper had been right to insist on calling them.

"I'm fine," Luke assured her again, but he wobbled a bit in the doorway.

She slid her arm around his back and helped him over the threshold. Then she closed and locked the door. Not that that would keep out Warren.

He knew the code.

How had she been so stupid?

And was she being that stupid all over again with Luke Bishop? She turned toward him then and found him staring at her.

"Please, stop beating yourself up," he implored her. "It's not your fault. None of this is your fault."

She nodded as if she agreed. But she didn't.

Luke pulled off his gloves and reached for her face, cupping it in his hands. "You are a smart woman, Aubrey Colton. You didn't fall for him…" He waited then as if he was afraid that she had; maybe he thought that was why she'd been reluctant to call the cops.

"No, I didn't," she said. "But I shouldn't have even gone out with him. I was a fool."

"Why?" he asked. "You didn't give him any money…"

"No, I didn't," she said. "When he started asking for it, I broke things off. I realized then that was his only interest in me."

"He's an idiot," Luke said. "You're so damn desirable. And you know you deserve better than Warren Parker." Then in almost a whisper he added, "I know that, too."

Was he implying that he wasn't better? Because he was…

He was so good that he was making her heart ache for him. And he was right there in front of her, his balance unsteady as he shifted all his weight to one leg. He swayed as if he'd been drinking, but she wasn't sure he'd even had a cup of coffee yet that morning.

"Come in here," she said, and she helped him over to the hearth. A fire had been lit there last night; it must have been how Warren had kept warm the night before. That and the blankets he'd left piled on the couch.

At least her ex apparently hadn't used her bed. She had never invited him to share it, and she certainly never wanted him to be there.

Not like she wanted Luke…

But he was hurt. She needed to focus on that now and not her attraction to him. "I'll start a fire while you get out of your snowsuit."

Fortunately Warren hadn't used all the wood that she had chopped and piled in a large crate next to the hearth. She was able to start a fire quickly, the flickering flames casting a warmth and a glow into the room and onto Luke. He'd unzipped and pushed his suit down, revealing his second layer of jeans and flannel shirt beneath them. The jeans were torn, just like the suit had been.

With the heat of the fire warming her, she shucked off her boots and suit as well. But she suspected it wasn't just the flames that warmed her but the memories that flitted through her mind from the night before, of what Luke had done to her, how he'd made her feel…

"You need to take off your jeans, too," she said. "We need to see how bad the wound is."

He wriggled his dark eyebrows at her. "You sure you're not just trying to get me out of my pants?"

She wouldn't mind; she definitely wouldn't mind. "We need to evaluate whether or not you'll need stitches."

"It doesn't matter if I do," he said. "We're not going to risk the roads and storm to drive to town, and you're not a doctor. Not that I'm opposed to playing doctor with you…" He wriggled his brows again.

And a smile tugged at her lips. "You're…"

"Incorrigible," he supplied when she trailed off.

That hadn't been the word she'd been about to use— she was going to say *wonderful*. But she didn't know if that was true; she didn't know if anything was true anymore. Her smile slid away, and she narrowed her eyes. "We need to at least clean up the wound," she said. "So drop your jeans."

"If you insist…" he murmured as he undid the button. Then he slowly—so very slowly—lowered the zipper.

The rasp of the metal echoed the rasp of the shaky breath Aubrey took. He pushed down the jeans, revealing the boxers he wore beneath them. As the denim caught on his lower leg, he grimaced.

Aubrey stepped closer and crouched down to inspect his wound. The snowmobile ski had ripped the material of his suit and jeans and some of his skin. But the scratches weren't deep; they'd already stopped bleeding, the dried blood sticking his jeans to the wound.

"I need to get your jeans off so I can clean your scratches," she said.

"Then do it fast like you're ripping off a Band-Aid," Luke agreed, and his jaw clenched as if he was gritting his teeth.

She couldn't bring herself to pull it hard, though; she didn't want to hurt him. So she started easing the denim away from his scratches, but he reached down and jerked it, then let out a low groan.

Blood started oozing again, streaking down his leg through the hair on his shin. "We need to clean this up," she said. "And get some bandages on it."

"Can I use your shower?" Luke asked.

And she remembered that day he'd been fresh from the shower when he'd caught her in his cabin. Desire choking her, she could only nod.

"It would be more fun if you joined me," he said but almost hesitantly as if he wasn't sure he should make the offer.

Or that she would welcome it?

She shouldn't, because she couldn't completely trust him. But then she might never be able to feel that way with anyone, not fully. She did trust, though, that Luke was a good man—one who pitched in and helped out, who cared about animals and people.

One who cared about her…

And she cared about him. Even if they had no future, even if he didn't intend to stay on in Blue Larkspur, she would always remember him. And she wanted more memories with him.

"The bathroom is this way," she said and started up the stairs that led to the second story of her home, which encompassed her master suite. As she'd hoped, the bed was made—the space untouched—and she was grateful that Warren hadn't been in her room.

She doubted, too, that he'd stuck around the ranch. If he believed they were going to call the police on him, he would have definitely found a way to get off the property—even if he had to drive the snowmobile to town.

"Are you okay?" Luke asked, as his hands settled on her shoulders.

She leaned back against him for a second before remembering that he was the one who was hurt—because of Warren Parker and because of her. And she jerked away from him. "Yes," she said. "Are you? How badly is your leg hurting?"

"Not so bad that I can't do this…" He leaned down then, scooped her up his arms and carried her into the adjoining bathroom.

"Luke!" she protested. She was too heavy for him—even if he wasn't injured.

But he didn't betray any weakness. All he betrayed, as he stared down at her so intensely, was desire. For her…

In the bathroom, he moved his hand from beneath her legs, so that she slid down his body. And through the thin material of his boxers and her jeans, she could feel his reaction to her closeness.

She was reacting as well—with a quickening of her pulse, with a pull from her nipples to her core. She'd never desired anyone the way she did Luke Bishop.

"We should shower," he said. "Clean up. Warm up…"

But instead of reaching for the faucet in the large walk-in shower, he reached for the buttons on her shirt and her jeans. He undressed her quickly; just as quickly she undressed him.

Then, naked and vulnerable before him, she shivered. And finally he reached inside the shower and turned on the faucet. While they waited for the water to warm up, he heated her with his gaze, running it hungrily over her.

"You are so beautiful…" he murmured. Then he leaned down and kissed her, and his mouth moved hungrily over hers.

Locked in each other's arms, they stumbled into the shower and under the warm spray of water. They bathed each other—with soap and caresses and then kisses.

There was a bench in her shower, and Luke settled her onto it before settling between her legs. He made love to her with his mouth, and as she screamed his name, he entered her. Then he tensed and groaned. "Condom…" he murmured.

Before he could pull out, Aubrey clutched him against her. "It's fine. I have an IUD and I've been tested."

"Me, too," he said then chuckled. "Well, not the IUD. But I've been tested." All soap and water, his skin was slick, her body wet as he slid in and out of her. And as he moved inside her, he kissed her and stroked her nipples, rousing her desire again, building that pressure inside her.

Until it broke and she screamed his name…

Then he tensed again, and his body shuddered as he found his release.

"Aubrey!" He uttered her name with awe and wonder.

And she felt the same—that what they shared, what they felt with each other was awe-inspiring. And even if it didn't last, that would be enough.

These memories would be enough—she hoped.

* * *

He shouldn't be here. Not in her bed after sex in the shower. Not in her home. But Luca couldn't bring himself to leave her even though he knew he should.

If the Camorra found him…

But maybe it was safer for her if he stayed—in case Warren Parker came back. What the hell was the man up to? And how the hell had he had the nerve to let himself into her house?

Luca could understand her ex not wanting to let her go, but the man wasn't going to win her back by manipulating and threatening her.

Even if Aubrey could be won back…

Once her trust had been broken, it was clear that Aubrey wouldn't offer it again. Which was yet another reason Luca knew he needed to leave.

He had been concerned earlier, when she hadn't wanted her brother to call the police, that she still had feelings for her ex. But it was clear that she'd been more worried about looking like an idiot than about the police arresting Warren Parker.

Warren deserved to be arrested, though. He needed to be locked up for threatening her.

"What's the matter?" Aubrey asked, her head on his chest. She must have heard the fast beating of his heart, or maybe he'd tensed with the anger coursing through him.

"I'm worried about you," he said.

She uttered a soft sigh that whispered across his bare skin as she murmured, "Me, too…"

He wondered if she was worried because of Parker or because of him. And he was afraid to ask.

A sound saved him from asking, though—the low rumble of an engine. It wasn't a car or truck, but a snowmobile.

Was it Warren?

Had he come after them? Luca released Aubrey and slid out of the bed.

"Where are you going?" she asked.

Hadn't she heard it?

"Someone's coming," he said. And he intended to be ready for whomever it was.

Jasper understood why Aubrey didn't want him to call the police on Warren. She was embarrassed, and more than that, she was probably concerned about the ranch as well.

How would a police report about a theft and a break-in affect their reputation? Would word get out? Jasper really didn't care about any of that; he cared instead about protecting his sister, his partner.

And once he'd left her alone with Luke Bishop, he had a strange feeling. Not so much about Luke but about Warren.

Where had he gone?

Had he left the ranch? Or was he just out there somewhere? And what did the man intend to do?

Had Warren fired those shots from the Sutherland property? Had he been trying to scare Aubrey or Luke? Or worse?

While Jasper had understood Aubrey's qualms about calling the police, he'd returned to the main lodge and done it anyway. If Warren had fired those shots, he was even more dangerous than Jasper had once thought he was. Then he'd considered the guy to just be a gambler and grifter. Now he realized that the man was capable of even more. Of theft.

Of attempted murder?

Unfortunately Jasper hadn't been able to convince the dispatcher that Warren posed an immediate danger, and with the storm having shut down the city, they hadn't been willing to spare an officer to come all the way out to the ranch to investigate someone taking a joyride on one of their snowmobiles. So, after making the call, Jasper had climbed back onto his machine to do a little investigating of his own.

Knowing that Aubrey and Luke had intended to return to her house to see if Warren had broken into it the night before, he'd headed in that direction. He hadn't gone far when he'd seen their tracks. At least sets that might have been theirs...

Theirs weren't the only ones, though.

Somebody had followed them. Had Aubrey and Luke noticed that they were being tailed?

Jasper couldn't tell. He could only speed up and follow the tracks to where they'd stopped—on the edge of the road that led to Aubrey's house. One snowmobile was parked in that area, and Jasper pulled his sled up next to it and killed the engine. Then he pulled off his helmet, so that he had better peripheral vision. And he peered around him.

Where had the rider gone? He studied the ground and found the bootprints deep in the snow that led from the abandoned snowmobile toward a stand of pines along the edge of Aubrey's yard.

A dark figure crouched beneath the boughs of one of the big pines, staring at the house.

Warren...

It had to be.

Jasper moved more quietly, more slowly—intent on sneaking up on the man, on catching him...

But he only made it a few feet before something struck him, knocking him into that deep snow, and everything went black.

Chapter 16

Where the hell had he gone? One minute Luke was in bed with her. The next he was nowhere to be found.

Would it be like that when he left for good? Aubrey had no time to ponder that. She quickly dressed and headed down the stairs just as the side door flew open, bouncing back against the mudroom wall. Two men stumbled through it, blood dripping from one of them.

She gasped at the sight of Jasper, leaning heavily on Luke, who had his arm wrapped around him. "Oh my God!" Her heart pounded hard with fear. "Are you all right?" she asked her twin.

Jasper squinted at her, as if his head was pounding as well as bleeding. Or as if he was struggling to focus...

How badly was he injured?

"Are you all right?" she asked again. "What happened?"

He grunted but nodded. "Yeah. Somebody hit me over the head…"

She turned on Luke. "Did you hit him?"

"Of course not!" he exclaimed. Then he half dragged, half carried her brother through the mudroom down the hall to the great room and the couch. "I found him lying in the snow like this…"

Bleeding. Injured.

With a grimace of pain, Jasper sank into the blankets Warren had left piled on the couch.

Her heart ached with pain and concern for her twin. "I'll call an ambulance."

"If I've got a pulse, they're not coming out—not with the mess the snowstorm caused," Jasper said. "The police wouldn't send anyone out to take a report about Warren stealing the snowmobile."

"But now that he hit you, they have to send someone out," Luke said, and he handed Jasper a towel he must have retrieved from the kitchen.

As Jasper pressed the towel to his head, he stared at Luke, his eyes narrowed now with suspicion, as if he doubted what Luke had said. Did he think that Luke was the one who'd struck him?

Luke shook his head. "It wasn't me. It had to be Warren."

"How?" Jasper asked. "He's the one I was sneaking up behind when someone whacked me over the head."

Aubrey gasped again. "What?" She looked at Luke hard, wondering, too, but then she shook her head. "No." No matter what his secrets were, Luke Bishop had no reason to hurt her brother.

Warren did, though, especially if he'd been worried

Jasper was going to hold him until the police arrived to arrest him.

"Are you sure it was Warren you were sneaking up behind?" she asked.

"Who else would it have been?" Jasper asked. "I saw a snowmobile from the ranch parked along the road and followed tracks up to your yard. Someone was crouching down by the pine trees, watching the house."

She shivered at the thought of someone being out there while she and Luke…

Her face got hot as embarrassment rushed over her. She and Luke had come here to see if Warren had broken into her house and to check his wound and then they'd wound up in the shower and then in bed.

Just as last night in the barn, they'd made a bed of blankets in the tack room. And she hadn't wanted to leave his arms then or now.

But Luke had had no such qualms of his own when he'd jumped up and rushed out of the bedroom. To strike her brother?

She shook head. "It doesn't make sense…"

"You said Warren has gambling debts," Luke reminded her.

And her embarrassment increased so much that she could only nod.

"Maybe someone is after him, trying to collect them," Luke suggested.

"And I got in the way?" Jasper asked and shrugged. "Makes about as much sense as any of this does." Then he turned toward Aubrey and asked, "Why does Warren think he's going to get money out of you?"

Because he thought she was so undesirable to any other man that he could manipulate her...

She wasn't about to admit that aloud, so she just shrugged.

"Because he's a fool," Luke answered for her. "Because he never really knew or appreciated you at all."

Was that how Luke really felt or was he the one who was trying to manipulate her now? Aubrey wasn't certain if she should believe him, but then she remembered how they'd just made love.

And she doubted that anyone could fake the passion that Luke seemingly felt for her.

The passion she felt in turn for him—so much so that she'd forgotten Warren was running around out there somewhere, desperate and dangerous, and apparently he was not alone.

But Jasper had been alone out there and could have died. "We need to get you to the ER," she insisted. "You need to have a CT scan, make sure that you don't have a concussion."

"I've got a hard head," Jasper said. "And you can't deny it since you tell me that all the time."

"You're the one who tells me that," she reminded him.

"That's because we're so much alike," he said and his lips curved into a slight, weak smile.

She wasn't so sure about that; Jasper certainly had had better judgment than she did when it came to relationships. Not that he'd had many, either, since they had always been so busy with the ranch. All their hard work had paid off, though. The place was a success; unfortunately, that had made her a target for Warren. And he just couldn't accept that he had failed to charm her.

"We need to get back up to the main lodge," Jasper said, "and make sure our guests are all safe."

Of course he would be worried about the business, just as he always had.

"My first concern is for you," she said.

"Same," he replied with a glance at Luke Bishop. Was Warren or Luke the reason he'd come out to her house to check on her?

"Let's get you up to the main lodge and we'll find out how the roads are and if we can get you into town," she said.

Jasper stood but wobbled slightly before Luke reached out and caught his shoulder to steady him. "Careful," he murmured.

"You're going to have to drive his snowmobile," she told Luke.

Luke nodded. "Fine. And we need to be extra careful on our way back to the lodge because he's still out there somewhere."

Jasper had already been hurt. Clearly, they were all in danger. Aubrey's shoulders drooped with the burden that it was her fault—because she'd had the bad judgment to date Warren Parker in the first place.

Had she fallen victim to her own bad judgment again over getting involved with a guest—with a man she barely knew?

Was Warren Parker the only danger? Or was Luke Bishop dangerous, too?

Luca didn't know what might have caused more damage to Jasper Colton—the blow to his head or clinging to Luca as he'd learned how to drive the snowmobile.

The man had been lucid enough to direct him with how to use the controls and where to go.

Aubrey had been following them, probably to make sure that she'd be able to notice if Jasper fell off. Luca hadn't liked her being back there; he'd worried that if someone shot at them again, she would be hit.

And she couldn't really be the target, could she? Warren wouldn't be able to get any money out of her if she was dead. The same of whomever Warren owed that money to...

They couldn't collect their debts from a dead man, either. So why would they try to shoot or kill people? Maybe that was why Jasper had been just knocked out, and why he wasn't dead.

When Jasper slid off the snowmobile back at the main lodge, he was steadier despite the way he flinched.

"You okay?" Luca asked him.

Jasper flinched again. "Yeah, now that that ride's over."

"Sorry." And not just about the ride...

Luca wasn't convinced that Warren was the one who'd hit Jasper or shot at them. Jasper had been sneaking up behind someone, so who had snuck up behind him? Who'd struck him hard enough to knock him out?

It made no sense for it to be someone Warren owed money to...

What made sense was that the Camorra had found Luca again and that this time they'd sent a couple of assassins after him. After the previous attempts on his life had failed, they probably weren't taking any more chances on his slipping away unscathed yet again.

But until they knew how bad the roads were, Luca

wasn't sure he would be able to go anywhere. He was trapped here...maybe with his would-be killers.

When he and Jasper and Aubrey walked into the lodge, everybody once again turned to stare. It probably wasn't because of Jasper—not with the way his blood had dried and blended into the strawberry blond color of his hair. Nobody had probably noticed that he was hurt...unless they were the one who'd struck him.

Luca peered around the room now, automatically dismissing the families. There were several of those in the great room, using tables to play games or put together puzzles while outside the snow began to fall again.

The wind wasn't hurling the precipitation at the glass with the velocity it had come down last night. The sparkly white flakes just drifted softly to the ground now, falling atop all that had already accumulated.

Just how long was this break in the storm supposed to last? Long enough for him to leave Gemini Ranch and Blue Larkspur?

But that meant getting someone from town to come out to pick him up. Unless he could drive Jasper to town in one of the ranch trucks. Surely they were four-wheel drive?

"You really should have a CT scan," he said. "Make sure that you don't have a concussion."

"I'm fine," Jasper insisted. "I just have a little headache. I'll take something for that and be back at it."

Aubrey studied her twin through eyes narrowed behind the lenses of her glasses. "Luke's right. You really should get checked out. I can drive you to town."

Jasper shook his head and flinched again. "We shouldn't both leave the ranch," he said. "Not with the storm starting up again. We don't want to get stuck in town."

"I can take you," Luca offered.

And Jasper narrowed his eyes now with suspicion. "No. I'm not leaving."

"Then at least let me get you the painkillers," Luca offered. "Where are they? Behind the desk?" He started toward the reception area at the front of the lodge. The computers were back there, the ones with all the guest records. He could find out who'd checked in recently, like after he'd made that call to Paolo.

Maybe Paolo hadn't given him up to the Camorra. Maybe he wasn't even aware that his phone had been tapped or his line recorded or...

Luca thought about his last conversation with Paolo, wondering if his cousin purposely kept it going, getting details out of him about where he was staying just as he had done every time Luca had called him before. He understood Aubrey's embarrassment and frustration over trusting Warren Parker.

Luca knew how it felt to trust someone you shouldn't have. He even understood her situation with her dad, now that someone he loved might have betrayed his trust, too.

"They're not back there," Jasper told Luca, stopping him from going any further.

"We have a small medical office in the lodge," Aubrey explained. "Usually it's staffed with a nurse, but since it's technically the off-season, she only comes in a few days a week."

"Is she here today?" he asked.

She shook her head.

But Jasper hesitated. "She might be here. She was here yesterday, and if the weather got too bad for her to leave…"

Like it had for Warren? Was that why he'd stayed in Aubrey's house? Because he hadn't been able to leave? Or was he hiding out from the people to whom he owed money?

No doubt the man was desperate; Luca understood that better than anyone. But was he dangerous?

Luca suspected there was someone far more lethal hanging around the ranch. Someone who'd been sent here specifically for him.

"Why don't you two see if the nurse is here?" he suggested. "Maybe a medical professional can talk him into going to the ER."

And even if she didn't, maybe Luca would have enough time to search through those guest records, to find viable suspects for the roles of Camorra hitmen…

Aubrey stared at him with suspicion, as if she knew he was up to something. "What are you going to do?" she asked.

He shrugged. "See what the chef has available to eat." His stomach grumbled at the thought of food, and he realized he hadn't eaten in a while.

But when she and her brother walked off, Luca didn't head to the kitchen. He headed instead to that reception desk. Whoever had been working it must have stepped away, and she'd left her computer unlocked. He didn't even have to figure out a password to pull up guest records. That could have been how someone had been able to search his cabin without breaking into it. Aubrey and whoever had searched his cabin the next day could have easily obtained the codes.

He scanned through the ones who'd checked into Gemini Ranch after Luca had placed that ill-advised call to his cousin. Even then he had already begun to suspect...

To wonder how the Camorra had tracked him down, despite the haphazard route he'd taken from Italy through Canada and then the northern United States to Colorado now. He knew all too well that Camorra methods were just as sophisticated as any other criminal organization's, so he'd been so careful, except for Paolo. He turned his attention to that guest list again.

One family and two couples had checked into the ranch after his call to Paolo. He dismissed the family, but one of these couples could be assassins the Camorra had hired.

His killers...

If they proved successful.

"This isn't the kitchen," Aubrey said.

Startled, Luca jumped and muttered an Italian curse. Being as distracted as he was—because of her—he wasn't certain he would be as lucky as he'd been when the Camorra had tracked him down in the past.

He wasn't certain that he would be able to escape.

"I was just looking for..." He floundered for an excuse.

"For what?" she prodded him.

She had to have noticed that he was on the computer, checking her guest records. He was surprised he hadn't felt her presence, like he felt it now in the quickening of his pulse, in the tightening of his muscles.

"I thought I recognized a couple who are sitting out in the great room," he said. "But I couldn't remember their names, so I pulled up the records to check."

She tilted her head then, studying his face. "You're not a good liar," she said. But rather than being angry with him for trying to tell her a falsehood, she seemed almost relieved.

"Why would I lie to you about this?" he asked instead. She was too smart to fall for it, just as she had been too smart to fall for Warren Parker's manipulations. She hadn't given him money, at least, but Luca was worried that the man had affected her self-esteem.

"Why would you lie to me, Luke?" she asked. "Why would you lie about anything? Who are you really?"

He wanted to tell her—so very badly—but even now he could feel that he was being watched. That *they* were being watched, and he didn't want to put her in any more danger than he already had. This was that sensation he'd noticed before—in those other cities—that had made him realize that someone had recognized him or been sent for him. That was how he'd managed to escape before getting hurt. With the blizzard trapping him at the ranch, escaping wasn't going to be easy.

"I don't know what you're talking about," he insisted, and he really wished that he didn't. That he was just a regular guest with no secrets, no assassins chasing him down everywhere he ran.

He wanted to stop running. He wanted to stay with her. But he forced himself to walk away now, toward the kitchen. "I really am hungry," he said.

"That's probably about the only truthful thing you've told me," she murmured.

He turned back then, at her words, and he reached out and trailed his fingers along her jaw. "It's not," he promised her. "Every compliment I've given you has been wholly deserved and entirely truthful. You're an amazing woman, Aubrey Colton."

And it was going to kill him to leave her. But better that he left than risk her getting killed with him. He would never forgive himself if he cost her her life or even her livelihood. He knew how much the ranch meant to her, how it was the realization of a dream she'd had since she was a child.

And if the same thing happened here that had happened at that hotel or at the B and B, Luca wouldn't forgive himself for that, either. And if they both survived, he doubted that she would ever forgive him anyway.

* * *

Is it over yet?

The text finally came through his phone, service temporarily restored. The service wouldn't last, though, not with the storm kicking up again.

Colorado…

He was not a fan. Not of this state, this country and especially not of this damn assignment. At least they were inside now, back at the main lodge, and he was able to sit near the roaring fire with the woman he'd hired to portray his wife. It had been cheaper to pay her than to cut his partner in on this job. Or so he'd thought…

He didn't know if this woman was really a wannabe actress. She was overplaying her role, which was annoying him so much that he would be relieved when he killed her. And he was going to have to do it eventually, just so that nothing could be traced back to him once he eliminated his target and collected the rest of his payment.

Aubrey Colton's ex-boyfriend was proving a pain in his ass, too. But he would pay for getting in the way—not with his life but with his freedom. He provided the perfect scapegoat for the murder of Aubrey's new lover.

Luca Rossi.

No.

Luke Bishop.

Nobody here knew him as Luca Rossi, not even her, he suspected. But it wouldn't matter what name they called him.

All that mattered, in the end, was that the man was dead. And it had to happen soon, before somebody noticed him following them around.

Luca scanned the great room then, and his gaze seemed to rest on him, like he knew.

Like he suspected.

From what he'd overheard, the others might have believed that dolt ex-boyfriend was responsible for the shooting the day before and for hitting the brother over the head…

But Rossi knew the truth. He knew that no matter where he went, the Camorra was going to track him down. They weren't going to forgive and forget about him.

They were going to have their vengeance. So—before he lost service again—he quickly texted back:

It will be over soon…

It had to be if he was going to escape as he had so many times in the past—if he was going to carry out his assignment and leave before suspicion fell on him. He had to act fast.

He had to kill Luca Rossi now.

Chapter 17

"You're sure you're really okay?" Aubrey asked her brother.

Jasper had insisted on talking to the nurse without her. That was why she'd returned to the front desk when she had caught Luke going through the guest records.

Had he really recognized someone? And from where?

"I'm fine," Jasper insisted. "The cut stopped bleeding, and I just have a small bump." He reached up as he said it and touched the back of his head, and then he grimaced.

Aubrey wasn't entirely sure she believed him. Just as she wasn't entirely sure she believed Luke about that couple. She glanced around the great room now, trying to figure out which one he might have recognized. Some of the couples had left, probably to return to their rooms after eating dinner.

Luke had eaten, like he'd initially claimed he had intended to. He sat at a table by himself. Aubrey ached to join him, and not just because she was hungry, too. In fact, she wasn't at all in the mood for food right now. Her stomach churned with nerves instead, over what could have been a near brush with death for her brother and with the fear that there might not be just a brush next time.

But would Jasper be the target again?

Or would Luke?

"I'm going to stay at the main lodge again tonight," Jasper said.

"That's a good idea," she agreed. That way, if he needed help because of the blow to his head, he would be closer to the nurse than if he was at his house.

"You should stay here, too," he told her.

"Why?" she asked. "I'm not hurt."

"Warren was at your place last night and earlier today," Jasper said. "He could have returned to it and be waiting for you to come back. You shouldn't be alone."

She didn't want to be alone; she wanted to be with Luke. But he hadn't asked her to join him for dinner. Instead he'd walked away from her as if he wanted some distance.

Could she blame him, with her ex-boyfriend acting so desperate and dangerous? But Luke wasn't the kind of person who seemed intent on keeping himself safe—not after he'd admitted to having researched dangerous people for his book. So she wondered if Luke was trying to stay away from her for his protection or for hers…

Which was silly speculation on her part. Probably something she wanted to believe just like she wanted to believe he was a good man and that all those compliments he'd given her really had been the truth.

"You need to stay, too," Jasper persisted. "It's too dangerous for you to go back to your house." He touched his head again, as if he needed to remind her of his wound.

She wasn't likely to forget that he'd been injured because of her. "I'm so sorry," she said.

He furrowed his brow. "About what?"

"About Warren," she said. "I had no idea when I first started going out with him what he was really like…" That his only interest had been in her money. He'd been so funny and charming when they'd first met at The Corner Pocket, a billiards bar in downtown Blue Larkspur. He'd challenged her to a game of pool with the loser having to buy dinner. He'd wound up paying that night. He wasn't a good pool player; at the time she'd thought he'd lost on purpose. Now she knew he was just that unlucky.

"I didn't see who hit me, so we don't know for sure that it was Warren," Jasper said. And he glanced across the great room at Luke now.

"I really don't think he had time to hit you and for you to have regained consciousness by the time he helped you into my house," Aubrey said in defense of her lover. She was worried that she was trying to convince herself of that as much as she was trying to convince her twin, though.

"He did help me," Jasper acknowledged. "I just think something's off about the guy."

"You liked him until Dominic talked to you," she reminded him.

"*You're* the one who talked to Dominic," he reminded her. "You're the one who asked our FBI agent brother to check up on a guest. Why, Aubrey? What's your interest in this guy?"

She shrugged. She couldn't say because she couldn't put it into words.

"You were the one who saw it first," Jasper said. "You noticed that there's something strange about him, something secretive, or you wouldn't have called Dominic."

"I shouldn't have," she said. Because Dominic had only raised more questions than he'd answered. More doubts. "A guest has a right to his privacy."

Why had Luke been looking at the guest check-in records? Was he really checking to see if he'd recognized someone? Or had he been looking for something else?

Luke stood up then, tossed some cash onto the table and headed toward the door. And he never once glanced in her direction while she had pretty much been staring at him the entire time.

Where was he going?

And why hadn't he talked to her?

Why hadn't he asked her to go with him?

Luca wasn't imagining it. Someone was staring at him. And it wasn't just Aubrey and her brother, though they'd been doing their share since they'd stepped into the great room. They stood together in the doorway, talking intensely.

About him?

He suspected it was. And he also suspected that whoever had really struck Jasper, whoever had really fired those shots, was watching him as well.

And he wanted that person—or people—far away from Aubrey. So he walked out without saying anything to her.

He wanted to make it clear to whoever was watching him that she meant nothing to him. Unfortunately, he was probably making Aubrey believe that, too. That he hadn't meant those compliments, that he wasn't starting to fall for her. He had meant them, and he was…

That was why he was determined to keep her safe, even if it meant he was risking his own life by going off on his own. But he wasn't unaware, like he'd been on those previous occasions.

After the Camorra had tracked him down in those other places, he now knew to be prepared. To be careful.

And he would have been if not for Aubrey, if not for being so damned attracted to the curvaceous blonde beauty. If not for her, he would have left Gemini Ranch already.

He should. But with the storm…

If the roads were unsurpassable for the police, no rideshare service or taxi would drive out to the ranch to pick him up. He should have rented a car; he would have if not for every company requiring a reservation with a debit or credit card. After he'd been tracked down before, he hadn't wanted to use those means of payment, hadn't want to lead someone to him. But he had anyway…

Or someone else, someone he'd trusted, had led that person here. Could his cousin have betrayed him like that? Even considering it made Luca feel as if he was the one hurting Paolo; he felt guilty even thinking it. He and Paolo had always been so close as kids, more like brothers than cousins. Paolo had been a lot like him in that he'd been easily bored, so he'd gotten into some scrapes growing up. He'd made some friends he shouldn't have, friends who'd been associated with the Camorra. But Luca had never suspected that Paolo would betray him.

When Luca stepped outside the main lodge, the wind struck him in the face like a hard slap. The cold air blasted him with icy bits of snow; these weren't the big flakes that had drifted down throughout the day. It was more like sleet now, cold and sharp and slippery.

His boot skidded off the first step and he nearly fell. But he righted himself and continued down the path that led toward his cabin. It was going to be a long walk that wound through the grounds and trees.

Maybe he should have borrowed one of the snowmobiles, like Warren Parker had. But with its loud engine, he wouldn't have been able to hear what he heard now. The sound of another door opening and closing, the crunch of boots on the snow. Someone was following him.

There were other routes he could have taken toward his cabin. One that led past other guest cabins. One that went by the barn…or this one…that led through the grounds with no one around to witness whatever was about to happen to him.

He had to get a few yards farther away from the lodge, from the main garden area, for darkness to swallow the light emanating from the building and the garden lights.

Once the light was gone, plunging him into blackness, he veered off the trail. Someone must have plowed the trail earlier, leaving the snow even deeper on the sides of it—so deep that he sank far into it and could barely move. But he forced himself through what felt like quicksand pulling him deeper, and he took cover in the trees on the edge of the trail. And there, hunkered down, he waited.

He wanted to know who'd been staring at him, who'd headed out right after him. Who was trying to kill him…?

Because he had no doubt that was why the person had followed him out of the lodge, to carry out what the Camorra had probably paid him or her or them to do.

Kill Luca Rossi.

The flight had been rough, the air choppy as the plane got closer to Denver, Colorado. A storm hung over the area, causing turbulence outside the plane.

Dread and fear caused turbulence inside it—and inside Paolo. What had he done?

And if it wasn't done…

If Luca wasn't already dead, he knew what the Camorra expected of him. They wanted him, instead of a failed assassin, to kill his cousin, figuring he might be the only one who could get close enough to Luca to carry out the hit on him. That was the only way they wouldn't call in the loans they'd given Paolo, the only way that they wouldn't kill him over his debts and over his cousin's exposé.

Luca hadn't called him, though. Had he figured it out? Or was he unable to call for another reason?

Because of this storm?

Or because he was already dead?

"We apologize for the rough landing," the pilot said over the speaker system. "The ground crews are struggling to keep the runways clear. We have to wait for a drift to be plowed before we can pull up to our gate and disembark, but you are now free to turn on your phones or other electronic devices."

His phone…

He'd turned it off as requested earlier. He reached into his pocket now and switched it on. It took a few moments before the screen lit up again.

And when it did, a breath of relief shuddered out of him. He'd been forwarded a text:

It will be over soon…

It had to have been sent earlier from the hitman to whoever his handler within the Camorra was. So maybe it was all over already.

Maybe Luca was already dead.

Chapter 18

Watching Luke leave made Aubrey feel even sicker with nerves and fear. For a moment—a long moment—she froze as those feelings overwhelmed her.

Then she realized what he'd done. He hadn't just walked away from her. He'd put himself in serious danger.

"He can't go off on his own like that," she murmured, and she started toward the door he'd left through just a short while ago.

Jasper caught her shoulder. "Why not?" he asked. "Why can't he go off alone?"

"Because Warren thinks Luke is my boyfriend," she admitted.

"Is it true?" Jasper asked. "Is he?"

Heat suffused her face, but she shook her head. "He's not my boyfriend."

That would imply that they had a relationship of some sort. And while they'd had sex, she knew it was only sex, and that it was not going to lead to anything but pleasure.

She'd thought that by having no expectations for anything else between them, she could avoid the pain. Now she wasn't so sure, because just watching him walk away from her without so much as a backward glance hurt. Badly.

She pushed her feelings aside now to explain to her twin. "Warren was hassling me a couple of days ago, and Luke interrupted and led Warren to believe that he was my boyfriend now."

"If that was so Warren would leave you alone," Jasper said, "it sure as hell didn't work."

"No," she agreed. "It actually seems to have made him more desperate and dangerous."

"So it really could have been him who fired those shots from the Sutherland property," Jasper said. "Maybe he was trying to hit Luke."

"He could have been," Aubrey agreed. Luke's reaction had been quick; he'd knocked her down as well. He might have saved her life.

But his was still in danger because Warren was probably out there somewhere, lurking around the ranch.

Waiting either at her house, like Jasper had said, or somewhere else on the ranch, like perhaps the path leading from the main lodge to the road to her house and Luke's cabin.

"We need to make sure Luke's all right," she said. Fear had intensified in her, knotting the muscles in her stomach, and she just knew that he wasn't…

That something had happened to him.

She rushed out the door then and nearly slipped off the steps. Jasper, who'd run out with her, caught her shoulder, like he had moments ago. But he didn't hold her back; he just steadied her.

Then they both walked down the stairs to the path leading away from the lodge. "Which way did he go?" Jasper asked as he peered through the snow.

It was falling hard and fast again, sheets of it slashing across Aubrey's face, chafing her skin. She should have gotten back into her snowmobile suit. But there wasn't time.

She knew that, even before she heard the grunts and blows of a fight.

"Over here!" Jasper yelled, and he headed down the path that led through the grounds and toward his and Aubrey's houses and Luke's very private cabin.

Once they were away from the lodge, the light evaporated—leaving such total darkness that Aubrey stumbled off the path. Her foot sank deep into snow, slowing her down, and Jasper rushed ahead of her. By the time she joined him—just a few yards down the trail—she couldn't tell apart the three shadows that grappled on the ground. Jasper must have joined the fight, but which man was he?

And which was Luke?

Then one of the figures jumped up and ran off, leaving just two tangled up in the snow. "I've got you!" Jasper yelled.

"You've got *me*," Luke remarked, his deep voice a rumble of frustration. "You let *him* get away!"

"Are you all right?" Aubrey asked as she rushed forward the last few steps. "Are you hurt?"

"No." But he didn't move from the ground; he stayed lying down for a moment.

Jasper scrambled up first, but when he started off after the man who'd run away, Luke jumped up and stopped him. "Wait!"

"But he's getting away. I *let* him get away."

Luke released a shaky breath. "No. He was bigger. Stronger..."

"Warren?" Aubrey asked with shock. Her ex was not bigger or stronger than Luke.

"It—it must have been his desperation, then," Luke said. "He was going to get away even before you showed up."

"Get away?" Aubrey asked. "Were you trying to catch him?"

"I heard someone following me," Luke admitted. "And I hid out in the trees until they showed up on the trail."

"And you tried to apprehend him yourself?" she asked with fear and awe. "You could have been killed."

"I'm fine," he said, but a groan slipped out of his lips as he moved.

"You're hurt." Or had his earlier leg wound been aggravated?

"That might be my fault," Jasper admitted. "I thought he had *you*. It looked like you were the aggressor."

It had probably looked that way because Luke had been trying to catch Warren. But had that really been Warren running off?

The guy had looked taller, broader…and just as Luke had claimed, stronger.

But there was no light out here, so maybe he'd just looked bigger in the dark. "We need to get back to the lodge," she said.

"I'm going to my cabin," Luke insisted.

"No," Jasper said. "Aubrey told me you pretended to be her boyfriend, so I think Warren's after you now. You can't go off alone. None of us can."

Luke shook his head. "No. It's too dangerous."

"It's too dangerous to be alone. He's not going to try anything in the lodge. There are too many other people around. And I'm calling the police again," Jasper said. "We need to find Warren and have him arrested or at least thrown off the property for trespassing—if we can't prove anything else."

"We can't really prove anything right now," Luke said. "I didn't get a good look at the guy I grabbed."

"Since he was following you and there are only our places out this direction from the main lodge, he must have intended to attack you," Aubrey said. "He must be who shot at us yesterday."

"Caleb has that gun," Jasper said. "He's probably already handed it to the police. We'll find out if it can be traced back to Warren. In the meantime let's get the hell back to the lodge."

Aubrey shivered then—from fear and from the cold. And an arm slid around her shoulders, pulling her close to the long, lean body of Luke Bishop.

He'd ignored her earlier, but now he must have noticed that she was freezing. "You don't have your snowsuit on," he said.

"Neither do you," she said. And his clothes were coated with snow from rolling around on the ground. "You must be freezing."

Jasper was beginning to shiver, too, so they all rushed back to the lodge, flinching at the sudden warmth inside after the cold.

"Get warmed up," she told her twin. "I'll show Luke to a room."

"I'll call the police again," Jasper said. "See if they can spare anyone yet to take a report."

"It's fine," Luke said. "Don't bring them out during a storm."

"It's not fine," Aubrey said. "You're hurt. Jasper was hurt. Warren needs to be stopped."

"Warren wasn't the one who hit me," Jasper reminded her.

"Somebody did. Somebody must be out there with him—helping him…"

"But there was only one man right now," Jasper said, and he turned toward Luke with a speculative look, like he wondered if Luke was the one who'd struck him.

Luke shrugged. "I don't know. There might have been two. I just managed to grab the one."

"And the other just let you do that?" Jasper asked.

"You guys showed up right away," Luke reminded him now. Then he shivered again.

The snow was starting to melt on his clothes, probably making him even colder as his skin got wet now, too.

She popped behind the reception counter and checked which rooms were available, jotting down the code for the lock of the closest empty suite. "I assume you already have a room," she said to Jasper, "since you stayed here last night."

He nodded and flinched.

"Go, get warmed up," she told him. "I'm going to show Luke to a room."

"What about you?" her brother asked.

She gestured at her clothes. "I wasn't rolling around in the snow. I'm fine." But she wasn't; she was shaken. If she and Jasper hadn't headed out after Luke...

He could have been hurt, or worse. Because now in the light, she saw a red mark on his jaw. Someone had struck him. Maybe even Jasper, when mistaking him for Warren.

"I'll get warmed up," Jasper said. "But I'm going to call the police again, too."

"You can wait until morning," Luke said. "Warren isn't going to try anything else tonight."

Jasper hesitated for a moment.

"You're the one who pointed out that the lodge is too crowded for anyone to try anything," Luke said. "We're safe here. Warren is the one in trouble, if he's out there with the storm picking up again."

"Okay," Jasper conceded. "We'll wait until morning before we call the police. Hopefully, they'll send someone out then to take a report."

Aubrey didn't feel so much as a pang of embarrassment now. She didn't care if everyone knew what a fool she'd been to date a man like Warren Parker. All she wanted was to make sure that he didn't hurt anyone she cared about again.

Like Jasper...

And Luke Bishop.

She waited until Jasper left them, waited until she'd opened the door to the vacant suite and followed Luke inside before she told him, "I'm sorry…"

"You're sorry?" he asked, his brow furrowing with apparent confusion. "You have no reason to be sorry."

"I understand why you want nothing to do with me, with the mess that's my life right now," she said. "I'm sorry that you've gotten involved in it."

He closed his arms around her then, pulling her tight against his tense body. His clothes were damp and cold, but still heat surged through her along with the passion she felt every time he touched her. Or got too close to her.

"None of this is your fault," he assured her. "*None* of it."

She released a shaky sigh. "Maybe you're right. I didn't make Warren the man he is—the gambler, the opportunist, but…"

"No buts," Luke said, and as if to stop her from saying anything else, he leaned down and covered her mouth with his then. He kissed her deeply—passionately.

And she knew that she'd been right earlier. He hadn't been walking away from her for his protection but for hers.

He could have been hurt. Had probably been, because when she closed her arms around his waist, he groaned. She jerked away from him. "Are you okay?"

He shook his head. "No…"

"Where are you injured?" she asked. And she reached for his clothes then, opening up his coat and pushing it from his shoulders. Then she reached for the buttons on his flannel shirt until it hung open over the thermal top he wore beneath it.

He reached for it then, lifting its hem to drag the shirt over his head. His ab muscles rippled when he moved, but then he grunted again. And she saw the marks from the blows he'd taken.

"You're hurt," she said again. "It looks like someone hit you really hard. You could have internal bleeding or broken ribs. You should see the nurse."

He shook his head as he tossed his shirts onto the floor atop his coat. "I don't need the nurse," he said, his blue eyes so dilated that they looked black. His expression was so intense that she shivered.

"What do you need?" she asked.

"You."

Then her clothes joined his on the floor until they were both naked, tangled in each other's arms. She tried to be careful, tried not to touch any of the red marks on his flesh, but he kept pulling her closer. Skin slid over skin; they moved together, breathed together, hearts beat together...

He lifted her then and stumbled back, tumbling onto the bed.

She started to apologize again, but he kissed her, sliding his tongue into her mouth. Then he moved between her legs, and after sheathing himself in a condom, he sheathed himself inside her. He filled an emptiness in her, an emptiness Aubrey hadn't even known she had.

His hands grasped her hips, and he murmured something—something in some other language, something sexy-sounding.

"What?" she asked.

"You're beautiful," he said. "So very beautiful..."

Her hair spilled around them both when she leaned

forward, when she pressed her mouth to his. She kissed him deeply and then she moved, rocking her hips back and forth, moving up and down.

He grasped her hips harder, driving her faster, driving her senseless. And he arched his back, contorting until his lips closed over one of her nipples. As he tugged on it, the pressure inside her spiraled out of control.

She bit her lip to hold in a scream of ecstasy as an orgasm shuddered through her. Then he tensed and groaned, his body convulsing beneath hers as he found his release, his pleasure.

What was this between them that any time they were alone they wound up making love? No. Having sex…

Was that all it was? Or had it already become more to Aubrey? Had it—and Luke Bishop—become an obsession?

Luca wanted to tell her the truth—so badly. Warren wasn't the one who'd followed him from the lodge. He wasn't the one Luca had grappled with on the path.

That man had been bigger and stronger than Aubrey's ex-boyfriend. He'd been bigger and stronger than Luca, too.

If not for Jasper and Aubrey coming along when they had, Luca had no doubt that the stranger probably would have overpowered him.

He was grateful they'd showed up and also scared that they had, because he was worried that they were in danger now. But surely Jasper was right, surely nobody would try anything at the main lodge with so many witnesses around?

He was holding on to the hope that Jasper was right,

as tightly as he was holding on to Aubrey, his arms wrapped around her as they lay beneath the covers of the king-size bed.

He closed his eyes for a moment, and behind his lids flickered the flames, the memory of the fire that had consumed that hotel in Wisconsin. There had been a lot of witnesses there, too, but that hadn't stopped the assassin they'd sent after Luca.

Luca couldn't endanger Aubrey's ranch and her life further. But he couldn't believe that the killer would take such a risk here during the storm. If he burned down the lodge, he'd have no place to go, either—not with the storm still raging outside.

The wind hurled bits of ice and snow at the windows, rattling the glass in the panes. The weather was getting worse, so the roads wouldn't be opening up anytime soon.

While the killer might have risked being witnessed, he wasn't going to risk freezing to death. He needed a place to stay as much as the rest of the guests. So the lodge was safe.

But Luca knew he wasn't.

And if Aubrey stayed with him, she wouldn't be, either. Luca had to leave her. He had to figure out some way to get off Gemini Ranch before she was hurt.

But the thought of leaving her made him ache.

He fumbled with a lighter, the flame flickering on and off. On and off...

He could do what had been done before. He could torch the whole place, if not to kill Luca Rossi, at least to flush him out.

Luca Rossi wouldn't get far, but neither would he—not with the travel advisories and whiteout conditions. The storm was raging again. Outside.

And inside of him...

The son of a bitch had jumped him. Had taken him completely by surprise.

If he'd seen him...

If anyone had seen him...

It didn't matter. They would die.

He glanced at the woman lying beside him. The actress...

Her eyes were wide open with shock. Her lips blue, her throat red from his hands.

Whatever she'd been, she was dead. He'd come back to the lodge in such a rage, furious that Luca Rossi—a worthless reporter—had gotten the jump on him.

Nobody had gotten away from him before. He was too good at what he did.

If he wasn't, he wouldn't have survived. He would have been arrested or worse...

He would have been eliminated, just as he'd eliminated the woman. The next person he eliminated had to be Luca Rossi...

Chapter 19

They had been trapped at the main lodge a couple of days now as the storm continued unabated. There hadn't even been another break like the one they'd got that morning when they'd met Caleb and Nadine at the Sutherland ranch.

Aubrey was worried about the storm. About the guests. About Warren. About her ranch.

But most of all she was worried that she was falling for Luke Bishop—even though she could see that he appeared disturbed. For the last couple of days he'd been pacing the suite, restless, on edge…

Maybe that was because he had stayed mostly in the guest room, even when she'd left to handle ranch business with Jasper. Not that she'd left him for long, since there hadn't been much to do, with everyone basically trapped at the main lodge.

Today, after all his pacing, he'd finally decided to head down to the dining room for lunch. He hadn't invited her along, but that was fine. She had things to do. And even though they'd parted ways when he went into the dining room and she'd walked away to the reception desk, his restlessness was inside her now, clawing at her. She was surprised, that after all the pleasure he'd given her over the past few days, she could have any tension left in her body.

But maybe that was why she was so tense.

So afraid...

Not of the storm but of her feelings. Those feelings were a distraction she couldn't afford right now.

At least the guests had food and the spa facilities to keep them busy.

Unfortunately, there were still the livestock to tend. And that calf. They hadn't found its mother, but it was doing well on a bottle and with the starter feed.

Kayla and the other hands had been taking care of the livestock. But with that disquiet inside her now, Aubrey stopped at the desk where Jasper was working. "I'm going out to the barn," she said.

She had to force herself to go. She would have rather stayed in bed with Luke than go out in the storm, than face the real world. But he wasn't in bed anyway. And even before he'd left for the dining room, he'd been pacing...like a caged animal. Like one just waiting for the opportunity to escape confinement.

Had she made him feel that way? Had being with her made him so tense and anxious?

"It's still nasty outside," Jasper warned.

She was afraid that it would have been nastier if she

and Luke had stayed in the guest room, if she'd given in to her frustration with him and demanded the answers he had yet to give her—about his past, about himself. Maybe that was why he'd left the room.

But the dining room was not far enough away for the space she needed, for the air she needed to clear her head.

She drew in a deep breath and reminded herself of the excuse she'd given herself for leaving the main lodge. "I need to check on that calf and make sure the horses are all being well tended."

Jasper furrowed his brow as he stared at her. "Really? You don't trust the hands?"

"Of course I do," she said. "But I told them to take a few hours off from the barn, and I would take care of the calf and the horses."

"You're getting fidgety," he said. "Me, too. It's like waiting for the other shoe to drop, waiting for Warren to show up again."

He hadn't. It had been two nights since he'd attacked Luke on the path. Or had Luke attacked him when he'd tried to catch him?

Maybe that had scared Warren off, because he hadn't made another appearance. Maybe he'd left the ranch that night. If he had, she doubted they would see him again.

He had to know by now that he had no hope of ever getting money out of her. The only reason for him to stick around would be to lash out in spite. To take out his frustration and his fear of his creditors on Luke.

Before she headed outside, she glanced into the dining room, looking for Luke. He was sitting at a table by himself. He had a plate of food in front of him, but it was untouched as he peered around, studying the other guests.

Was it his writer's curiosity that had him so interested in everyone else? Or was he looking for that couple he thought he'd recognized?

There was only one couple in the dining room now, and a few single men sitting alone like Luke was. They must have lost their spouses to the spa.

Maybe Aubrey would make use of the facilities herself, after she returned from the barn. She could use a massage or a steam.

But neither of those would release her tension like Luke did. He was such an amazing lover, so thorough, so generous.

So addictive.

That was the problem. The more time she spent with him, the more she craved him. But she knew, from his restlessness, that he was anxious to move on. And she had no doubt that once the roads were cleared, he would be gone.

She drew in a shaky breath and forced herself to head toward the outside door. "You're not walking," Jasper called after her.

She shook her head. "No. I'll take a snowmobile." She hurried outside to the building where all the equipment was kept. The snowmobiles and ATVs and skis. Maybe she should have strapped on some cross-country skis and headed to the barn that way. The wind wasn't howling as loudly as it had been.

And the snow wasn't falling as thick.

Either this was another break or the storm was ending. And that meant that Luke would be leaving. So she intended to make just that quick snowmobile trip out to the barn and back.

Before he was gone…

But as she drove off, she had this strange sensation—fear that she might not have the chance to see him again.

Standing outside the lodge, Luca watched Aubrey leave. And he forced himself not to call out to her. Not to stop her.

It wasn't that he didn't want her to go. It was that he *was* going, and he was tempted to tell her goodbye. But he didn't trust himself to actually follow through and leave her if he was alone with her again. Because every time they were together, they wound up in each other's arms.

He'd never experienced such passion before—from anyone else or from himself. He'd never wanted anyone as obsessively as he wanted Aubrey Colton. But it wasn't just desire he felt for her. He admired her, too. He respected everything she'd accomplished.

She was so smart, so hardworking, so straightforward, and she deserved someone who could be as straightforward and honest with her. That was why Luca had to leave.

Just his presence near her put her and her ranch in danger. He had to leave. The weather was letting up now.

Aubrey had put on a snowsuit and taken off on the snowmobile, and he intended to do the same. But instead of heading toward the barn, like she had, he planned to travel toward town. He wouldn't wait for someone to clear the roads; he would snowmobile to town and take a bus out of Blue Larkspur. He had no idea where he would go; he knew only that it had to be far enough away from Aubrey that she wouldn't be hurt.

But the thought of leaving her made him ache…

He already felt hollow and empty inside, but he had no choice. He'd felt it again in the dining room, the intensity of someone's stare, their animosity toward him.

Their restlessness…

Whoever had been sent here to take him out wasn't going to wait much longer to act again. Not now, when the storm was letting up again.

So Luca had to leave while he could.

He couldn't leave without the things he'd left in his cabin, though. His fake identification and passport. His money. His laptop. His notes.

So once he put on the snowmobile suit and found the keys, that was where he headed first, along the path where he'd fought with his attacker.

His bruises were just beginning to turn from purple to yellow now, but his ribs were still tender. The man with whom he'd struggled that night definitely hadn't been Warren Parker, so it had to have been one of the other guests.

Or maybe a ranch hand…

He should have asked Aubrey if they'd hired anyone new sometime after he'd checked in, after he'd talked to Paolo. Paolo had to have given him up. His cousin had to be the one who'd helped the Camorra find him everywhere he'd gone to hide from them. Luca had been too careful, too paranoid about the power and the reach of the Camorra to betray himself with using the credit cards too often. He hadn't realized that the Camorra would be able to get to someone so close to him, to someone he'd considered a brother.

His heart ached with the betrayal. He wanted to make excuses for Paolo, wanted to believe it was only because he'd been threatened that he'd given up Luca. But he'd had the opportunity to leave, like Luca's mother and aunt. Paolo hadn't wanted to give up his business or his friends and family, though.

Luca had understood. He didn't want to spend his life like this, running from place to place. Isolated from everyone he cared about. But he had no choice if he wanted to stay alive and to keep everyone he cared about from getting hurt.

That was why he couldn't talk to Aubrey, couldn't ask about her employees and shouldn't have asked about her guests. But she'd caught him searching the records. There had been two couples who'd checked in after he'd talked to Paolo. And both of the men from those couples had been eating alone this morning. Both of them had been watching him…

With ordinary curiosity or that hostility he'd imagined?

He shivered now as that feeling swept over him again, like the snowmobile swept along the path. The path ended at a fork. The road to the left led to his cabin, and the one to the right led to the barn. That was probably where Aubrey had gone, to check on the calf. He wanted to follow her there, so badly that he began to turn the handlebars in that direction—to the right.

He wanted to see her again—just one more time, wanted to kiss her lips, touch her silky skin. He knew they'd be alone; he'd heard Kayla and some of the other hands in the dining room planning on using their employee discount for spa services for a massage and a steam.

So he would be able to have a private goodbye with Aubrey. That longing pulled at him so hard that he lowered his head to draw in a deep breath. And something whizzed past his head just as the sharp sound of gunshots rang out.

Somebody had followed him from the lodge and was shooting at him now.

He should have waited.

Until he had a better shot.

Or until Rossi had headed back to this cabin. But when he'd stopped at that fork and seemed to point the snowmobile in the direction of the barn, he'd panicked.

Rossi had gotten away from him too many times. And he'd known why the guy had hopped on the snowmobile. Rossi had seen the break in the storm as an escape.

But he couldn't escape death.

Not again.

Not as he had so many times before.

So he'd raised his gun, the Glock he'd brought since he'd left his long gun in the abandoned barn, and he had started firing.

But Rossi had lowered his head just enough that the bullet had missed. Though maybe the helmet would have protected him anyway.

He raised his gun and focused again at Rossi's back, aiming the barrel right between the man's shoulder blades. This time he couldn't miss.

Chapter 20

The horses reared up, pawing at their stall doors as sudden gunshots reverberated outside the barn. Warren must have come back. And with another weapon...

Aubrey ducked down but no bullets whizzed past her. Despite the volume of the sound, they weren't close. Yet.

But they must have been heading toward her direction. Aubrey ran out of the stall where she'd been playing with the calf, across the barn toward the tack room. She pushed open the door and rushed over to the cubby that had a door and a combination lock on it. Her fingers shaking, she fumbled with the tumbler until finally it clicked and the door opened.

She reached inside and pulled out a gun. Every ranch had one to protect their livestock and occasionally to protect themselves. Aubrey knew how to shoot, but she'd never had to use it for her own protection before.

Until now…

The gunshots had stopped, but now she could hear the rumble of snowmobile engines until that sound died, too. Had whoever been driving them died as well?

But then there was another noise, barn doors crashing open before slamming shut again. She rushed out of the tack room then, gun raised, and stared down the sight on it.

At Luke Bishop.

But she didn't lower the barrel. She held it on him, and her voice vibrating with nerves and fury, she asked, "What the hell is going on?"

She didn't believe the culprit was Warren—not now. Not when he'd had days to get away, to get over whatever irritation or resentment he'd felt about Luke.

No. It wasn't Warren who'd fired those shots at Luke. There was someone else who wanted him dead. And she damn well wanted to know why.

This was the second time in a short while that someone had held a gun on him. The first time, the person had fired so many times that the shooter had had to stop somewhere to reload the weapon.

So Luca had fled to the barn. He regretted that he'd led danger right to Aubrey, but if he was going to survive, he needed a weapon. And she'd mentioned that ranchers always had guns.

She hadn't carried one on her when they'd been moving the cattle, so he'd assumed it was in the barn somewhere.

Now he knew where—trained right at him.

"What's going on, Luke?" she asked again, her voice raspy with anger and fear.

"Somebody's shooting at me," he said.

"Why?" she asked. "And you damn well better tell me the truth."

"There's no time," he said with a nervous glance over his shoulder. He'd secured the doors with the big wooden slat they'd slid over them the other night to keep out the wind and snow. But he doubted that the board would keep out the killer. "He's out there." But that wasn't where he was going to stay. "He had to see where I went."

And that was why Luca shouldn't have come here.

"I know how to shoot," she said, her voice strong and steady—just like she was. "Let him come. I just want to know who the hell I'm shooting."

Luca shivered then because it was clear that she knew it wasn't Warren who'd chased him into the barn. And her dark blue eyes had gone icy with that knowledge and with suspicion of him.

He glanced over his shoulder at those doors. They weren't moving—nobody was trying to get in. Yet. But he knew that the assassin would try soon. Luca knew that the Camorra did not give up.

Ever.

"We need to hide for now," he said. "Please, Aubrey, for your sake as much as mine."

She stared at him for another long second before she finally lowered the gun barrel. Then she turned and headed down the wide aisle between the horse stalls, past the tack room, until they reached a ladder at the end of it. "Up here," she said.

The open loft was probably a safer hiding place than the tack room. From this vantage point, they would be able to see when the assassin got into the barn. Unless he waited outside for them to leave and intended to pick them off then.

"You first," Luca said, making sure that she headed up the steps and got to the relative safety of that loft before he did.

With her gun under one arm, she climbed the ladder. Then she looked down at him as if she expected him to run. But he was already climbing up to join her among the bales of hay.

They weren't alone up there. Soft mewing noises drew their attention to where the cat—the gray tiger-striped tabby that had cuddled with the calf—snuggled with the kittens she nursed. There were at least five of them, so new that their eyes weren't even open yet. A couple of black ones, two dingy white and a little orange one. There might have been three of the black ones; they were pressed so close together, fighting over the teats on their dam's belly, that it was hard to tell.

"Oh, Mama," Aubrey murmured. "This isn't a safe place for you."

"It's not safe for you, either," Luca warned her.

Aubrey patted the stock of the gun. "I'll be fine. Once you tell me the truth."

"I can't..." he murmured. "Not without putting you in more danger."

She arched a blond brow above the rim of her glasses. "More? I'm in danger, Luke, and I deserve to know why. I deserve to know what you did that you're hiding out from someone."

"You're right," he said. Despite his best intentions, he had put her in danger. And she did deserve to know. "I'm hiding from the Camorra."

Her brow furrowed. "Camorra?"

He nodded. "It's an Italian organized crime group that is very prominent in Naples and controls a portion of Italy."

"What did you—did you testify against them? Did you…" Her voice cracked and she swallowed hard before continuing, "…did you *turn* against them?"

His heart ached at what she thought of him, that she wondered if he could have ever been part of such an organization.

"God, no," he said. "I never worked for them. I was investigating them. I am a writer, Aubrey, like I said. My name is Luca Rossi."

Usually people recognized his name. He'd done more articles than the one about the Camorra. But then, Aubrey was always so busy with the ranch that she might not have heard of him.

But a soft gasp slipped from her lips, and she nodded in sudden realization. "Yes, I remember now. The news outlets here in America picked up the story, too, about what you'd done, how many people your investigation helped authorities convict and send to prison."

"Not enough," he murmured. "Not all of them. They're still after me, Aubrey. That's why I've changed my name, why I pay cash, why I try to stay away from people."

But it hadn't worked. He hadn't been able to stay away from her. And now, because of his selfishness, his weakness, he would probably lose her…even as he lost his own life.

* * *

"What's missing?" Jasper asked the housekeeper, who'd stopped him just as he was about to leave the main lodge.

"All the sheets from suite 202."

The snow had stopped but for an occasional flake and the wind was no longer howling, but travel was still not advised. "Have the guests checked out?" he asked.

Occasionally people packed up the linens and towels when they left, either for souvenirs or because they somehow believed they'd paid for them.

The housekeeper shook her head. "And we actually screwed up when we let ourselves into the suite. The guests had requested a Do Not Disturb order on it. We weren't supposed to go inside, but the maid cleaning that floor didn't pay attention. And when she went into the room, she thought it was very strange that the bed had been stripped already."

It *was* very strange, especially since the guests had not checked out.

"She found something else, Mr. Colton," the housekeeper continued.

"What?" he asked.

"Gun cases." And now she shuddered.

"Gun cases?" he repeated.

"Yes, you know the ones that have the molds inside that hold the weapons," she explained.

And Jasper's heart sank with the possible implications of that.

Nobody had signed up for hunting at the ranch. That wasn't something they offered, so why the weapons? Had one of those cases belonged to the gun Caleb had found on the Sutherland property? Had their guest been responsible for firing those shots?

Maybe Warren Parker hadn't had anything to do with that weapon or with those gunshots. Or maybe even with hitting Jasper over the head...

The front door opened with a blast of cold air, and Kayla St. James ran into the reception area. "Jasper!" she exclaimed, and there was something almost like relief in her voice. But then she rushed on, "I heard gunshots between here and the barn, and I saw two people racing toward it on snowmobiles."

Jasper reached for her, gripping her shoulders. "You're okay?"

She nodded, and her ponytail bobbed. "Yes. I turned around and headed back here to call the police. But I don't think they'll be able to get here in time to stop whatever's going on, to protect Aubrey..."

His stomach lurched with a sickening surge of fear. "Aubrey's in the barn." She'd gone out there to check on the calf and the horses.

And Luke Bishop had headed out not long after she'd left. He must have been going out to join her. And somebody was chasing him and shooting at him.

Who the hell was Luke Bishop? And was he going to get Aubrey killed?

Chapter 21

Everything Luke—no, Luca—had told her ran through Aubrey's mind. The Camorra...

They were a dangerous, far-reaching criminal organization. And he was the journalist who had recently exposed criminals at every level of local Neapolitan life as well as their connections within the government—corrupt officials who'd been taking bribes and kick-backs. Luca had disappeared shortly after his story ran, and most people believed he'd been killed as retribution.

She hadn't considered that that man could still be alive and that he could be her lover. But it all made sense...except for one thing.

"Why didn't you tell me?" she asked.

"I didn't want to put you in danger," he said.

The big doors of the barn rattled, and she knew that he was right. She was in danger.

But it didn't have anything to do with knowing the truth. Knowing the truth might have made her more prepared. Because now she knew it wasn't Warren coming after Luke, after both of them.

It wasn't some bungling gambler acting out of desperation. It was a hired, professional killer. She handed the gun to Luca. His eyes widened as he stared down at it.

"What are you doing?" he asked.

"Trusting you." And that damn well wasn't easy for her, but she didn't see any reason for him to be lying. She rushed over to the door of the loft that opened to the outside.

"Isn't it too high to jump out?" Luca asked.

But she didn't open the door. She grabbed the rope that was looped up beside the window and pulled it free of the pulley above it. That was how they hoisted up bales of hay from the wagon they would park below it.

She didn't want to hoist anything now. She intended to rope it.

"What are you going to do with that?" he asked.

"I'm better with a lasso than I am with a gun," she admitted.

"But, Aubrey—"

"Can you shoot?" she asked him.

He looked down at the gun now, undid the safety and lifted the butt of the weapon to his shoulder. "Yes."

"Good," she said. "Because he's coming…"

The board that held those doors closed broke, and the doors banged against the walls as the snowmobile plowed through them. The man stopped the machine just inside and climbed off it. He wore his helmet with a snowmobile suit. He could have been anyone, but from the way he held his gun, it was clear what he was.

He'd come here to take out Luca.

And Aubrey wasn't going to let that happen. She whirled the rope around her shoulders. The guy must have heard it, because he looked up, and as he did, he brought up the barrel of his gun and pointed it into the loft.

Aubrey tossed the rope, dropping the circle over the guy's arms. As she pulled it tight, he started firing.

Closer gunshots echoed, as Luca fired back. Then the guy fell onto his back on the ground, the weapon down at his side. Aubrey tried to tighten the rope more, tried to link the guy's arms together, but he was too heavy, like dead weight.

"I think I got him," Luca murmured, but his voice was a whisper, like he didn't dare let the man hear that he was alive. That the shots he'd fired wildly, because of the rope tightening around his arms, had missed.

Had they missed?

Aubrey stared at Luca, looking for any sign of blood. But he seemed fine. As did the mother and kittens he stood in front of, as if he'd been protecting them with his body—like he'd protected her that day in the pasture when those shots were fired.

Naively she'd thought then that he was overreacting. Now she realized how wrong she'd been, and how much danger he'd been in this entire time.

Was that threat gone?

The man lay yet on the floor below them, perfectly still. He had to be at the very least unconscious. At the most...

She shuddered and started toward the ladder. But Luca caught her arm.

"Stay up here," he said. "Let me check."

Aubrey reached for the gun he held. "I'll hang on to this," she said.

"I thought you trusted me," he said.

"You might shoot yourself in the foot trying to get down there with a loaded gun."

And if the man was conscious, he might shoot Luca in the back as he descended the ladder. She raised the butt back to her shoulder and stared down the barrel at the hitman lying on the floor.

Had he moved?

Was he twitching?

Her heart pounded hard with fear. "Luca…" she murmured in warning. "Be careful."

But it was already too late. He was already halfway down the ladder. His back exposed to the man who lay on the ground.

When she'd picked up the gun, she'd dropped the rope, so it could have loosened around the man's shoulders, could have made it easier for him to aim his gun and fire.

If he was just faking being unconscious, if he was just wounded instead of dead…

And if he was, then he was about to have a clear shot at Luca. Aubrey had a clear shot at him, though, down the sight on the barrel of the shotgun.

Could she do it? Could she shoot another person if she had to? Even for Luca…

Luca eased slowly down the ladder from the loft to the barn floor. It wasn't that he was afraid of the man lying on the ground—because he was pretty sure that one of his shots had struck the assassin. If not for Aubrey, Luca would have been dead already. She had thrown the rope around the killer's arms, making it impossible for him to aim and shoot. But the guy had fired a lot of shots wildly…

The mama cat and her kittens were fine, though. Luca had made certain to stand between them and the gunfire, and he'd fired back at the assassin. He'd only ever fired a gun at targets on a range—never at another human being. But he'd known that if he hadn't, the man wouldn't have stopped after shooting Luca; he would have killed Aubrey as well.

Luca's heart pounded fast with the fear he'd felt, the fear that she might have been hurt. But she was fine. He glanced up at the loft just to make sure and found her holding tightly on to that gun.

Had he left any bullets in it? Would she be able to use it if she needed to?

What if this hadn't been the only killer sent for him? What if, as Luca suspected, the guy didn't work alone?

Where was the woman who'd posed as his wife? Because surely, this person had to have been one of the couples who'd checked in after Luca made that call to his cousin.

After he stepped from the last rung of the ladder onto the concrete floor of the barn, Luca glanced back to the doors of the barn that the snowmobile had broken open. Nothing but snow, just a few fat flakes, swirled around outside.

Inside the horses whinnied and pawed at their stalls, agitated from all the chaos. Their hearts probably pumped as hard with fear as Luca's had, as it still did.

Because even if this man was dead, Luca knew it wasn't over. The Camorra would send someone else for him—if they hadn't already. But as he turned to check on the man, he saw the shooter lift himself up, manage to raise the barrel and squeeze the trigger of his gun one more time.

The shot reverberated throughout the barn.

It had taken a couple of days for him to get from Denver to Blue Larkspur—because of the storm. Finally it had let up and the roads were clear enough for travel, and Paolo's cab pulled up outside a hotel. As the van stopped at the curb, police vehicles sped past it, lights flashing and sirens wailing.

"What's going on?" he wondered aloud. They could have been responding to anything—an auto accident, a fire...

But he had a strange sensation in his stomach, a mixture of nerves and dread. Over the past couple of days, he hadn't had any more communication from the Camorra.

He hadn't known what was going on—what *soon* had actually meant. Was it over yet?

The cabbie tapped one of his ears, in which he wore an AirPod. "According to the police scanner, there's been a shooting out at the Gemini Ranch."

It had to be over now. Luca had to be dead. He thought about telling the cab driver to turn around, to bring him back to the airport, so that he could go home.

But he needed to make certain—for his sake more than anyone else's—that Luca was really gone. Because if Luca wasn't dead, Paolo couldn't go home until he proved that he was…

And to do that, he might have to actually kill his cousin himself.

Chapter 22

He was dead.

Aubrey hadn't had time yet to process everything that had happened. One minute the barn was ringing with gunshots; the next minute police and ambulances were swarming the property.

The ambulances had been too late to save him. She wasn't sure which shot had killed him—the one she'd fired when he turned his gun on Luca. Or any of the ones Luca had fired when the man first burst into the barn.

Either way, the hired assassin was dead, and unfortunately, his hadn't been the only body found on the property of Gemini Ranch. When the police had conducted a search, they had found a woman's body partially buried in the snow just off the path that ran between the main lodge and the barn. She'd been strangled to death.

Aubrey shivered at the thought of a murder taking place on the ranch. The woman's body had been wrapped in bedding that had gone missing from a guest room at the main lodge, which the hired killer had rented.

Aubrey wasn't at the ranch now. The police had separated her and Luca at the barn, driving each into town in separate vehicles to the police department to give their statements. Like they were the criminals.

Even if her shot had killed the assassin, it had been to save Luca. And if one of the shots he'd fired had killed the man, then it had been in defense of both of them. The thought of taking a life—anyone's life—had regret and pain swirling inside her, making her nauseous, yet she knew she'd had no choice. But death...

Hers and Luca's, because the assassin would have killed them both.

The police hadn't questioned them for long before they were free to go. But neither of them had been ready to return to the ranch, where they'd nearly lost their lives—where two other people had.

So they'd taken a room at one of the nicer hotels in Blue Larkspur, and Aubrey stood at the window of the room now, staring out at the street below. The snow had been cleared away, and what hadn't been plowed had begun to melt.

The storm was over.

Strong arms closed around her, and she was pulled up against a hard male body. "Are you okay?" Luca asked.

Too overwhelmed to speak, she could only nod.

He leaned down, until his face was against her cheek,

his stubble rubbing sensuously against her skin. "I'm sorry," he murmured. "I'm so very sorry…"

"For what?" she asked.

Now that she knew who he was, she knew what he'd done—how he'd worked to take down an organization of killers and criminals and exposed the corruption in government and law enforcement across a country.

"I am so very sorry for putting you in danger," he said. "That was the last thing I wanted. That was why I didn't want you to know the truth. In case they came looking for me…" He shuddered. "I didn't want them to think you would know where I was going. I didn't want you to get hurt because of me."

She turned toward him then. As much as she respected what he'd done as a journalist, she wasn't thrilled with how he'd treated her—no matter what his reasons were.

"I did get hurt," she admitted. "I blamed myself for the danger—that it was Warren—and you let me think that."

He flinched as if she'd slapped him. "I'm sorry. But I didn't know for certain that it wasn't Warren who'd been shooting at us. He'd been hanging around. I wanted it to be him rather than that I had been found again."

A pang of panic struck her heart. "Again?"

"This wasn't the first attempt on my life since I've gone into hiding," he replied. "It seems like they always find me no matter where I go…"

She flinched now—because she knew what that meant. That he wouldn't be able to stay…

Not in Blue Larkspur and not at the ranch, because the Camorra already knew that he was here. And when they didn't hear back from the assassin they had sent, they would undoubtedly hire another one for Luca Rossi. Or Luke Bishop, since now they probably knew what he was calling himself.

"That's why we're here," she said, realizing why they hadn't returned to the ranch. "That's why you wanted to check into the hotel. You're going to leave."

He drew in a shaky breath and nodded. "While I was being questioned, a certain US marshal and FBI agent called in with the offer of new credentials for me, a new place to go…"

A pang struck her heart. "Dominic? Alexa?"

He nodded.

Were they helping him? Or her? Did they want him far away from her to protect her?

Probably.

But they couldn't protect her from the pain she was feeling. The pain that she would feel when he left. He was here now, though—with her. And she intended to make the most of that, the most of being with him.

"How long do we have?" she asked.

"Tonight," he said. "Tomorrow I have to leave."

She nodded and said, "Then let's make the most of tonight."

"You're not going to argue with me?" he asked.

"Why would I do that?" she asked. "I understand." His life was in danger—would probably always be. "I would offer to go with you, but—"

He pressed his finger over her lips. "You can't. You have the ranch. Your family. I understand."

That was what made it so hard—that she didn't think

she would ever find anyone else like Luca, anyone with whom she could connect on so many levels.

She forced a smile for him. "Then I think we both understand what tonight is…"

Goodbye.

"A gift," he said. "Every minute I get to spend with you is a gift."

She smiled at his sincerity and at the sentiment. That was how she would look at it, too. With gratitude…

His breath shuddered out in a ragged sigh. "You are so beautiful…"

Usually she would have protested his compliment—because she wouldn't have believed it. Despite her knowing what he was doing, she had to admit that Warren's manipulations had affected her self-esteem, had brought back all that childhood teasing and bullying.

But now…

With the way Luca looked at her, his face flushed with desire, his beautiful eyes dilated with it, she had no doubt that he was sincere.

She *was* beautiful. And she would never doubt it again.

"And you are so strong and so sexy," he continued.

She was strong; she knew that. But she didn't know if she was strong enough to survive this—to survive his leaving. But she pushed that worry from her mind, too.

All she wanted was to focus on the gift that this evening was, that Luca Rossi was.

"You are beautiful," she told him, her heart filling with warmth—with an emotion she didn't dare to identify or acknowledge. He wasn't just beautiful on the outside but on the inside as well, with his care for the calf and the mother cat and kittens.

Luca chuckled over her compliment. "I am going gray," he said, and he reached up to run his hand over the stubble on his jaw.

"It's sexy," she assured him.

He grinned, then looped his arms around her, pulling her against his body. "You're the sexy one. The things you do to me just when I look at you…"

With him holding her as close as he did, she could feel the things she did to him, the physical reaction he had to her. She arched her hips and rubbed against the fly of his jeans, teasing him.

This time his chuckle sounded gruff. "Aubrey…"

Her skin tingled at the way he said her name, with passion in his voice. Then he lowered his lips to hers, and that passion was in his kiss, in the way he made love to her mouth.

Now she tingled everywhere, her nipples taut and sensitive against the cups of her bra. Desire pulled at her, making tension spiral inside her. "Luke… Luca…"

Luca fit him better, fit the accent and the man. Tonight could be the last time anyone ever called him that, which was sad. But Aubrey refused to let sadness anywhere near her right now. She wanted only him near her—inside her.

He must have felt the same, because his hands moved to her clothes, peeling them off her body. Once he had her naked, he carried her to the bed and laid her on the plush mattress. Instead of joining her, he just stood there, staring at her as if he wanted to memorize what she looked like.

Then he stepped closer, and he ran his hands over her, as if he wanted to memorize how she felt. And then he was tasting her...

His lips glided across every inch of her skin, lingering on her neck where her pulse jumped and the curve of her breasts before pulling gently on her nipples.

She moaned and reached for him. "Luca..."

But he moved farther down her body, and with his lips and his tongue, he built the pressure inside her even more.

She arched and squirmed on the bed, wanting more, needing more...

But he pulled back, chuckling. He was teasing her. Torturing her.

"Luca..." It wasn't a plea now but a warning. She could torture him, too.

Ignoring the throbbing low in her body, she reached for him, pulling him onto the bed with her. Then she unzipped his jeans and released his straining erection. And she teased him with her lips and her tongue...until his control snapped.

His hands shaking, he fumbled a condom packet from his jeans before ripping it open with his teeth. He sheathed himself. Then he was inside her, moving, thrusting, and the pressure broke. An orgasm gripped her with such overwhelming pleasure that tears streamed from her eyes as her body shuddered. Luca's body tensed as he joined her. But then he was shaking, his hands stroking her face, wiping away her tears.

"Did I hurt you?" he asked, his voice gruff with concern and regret.

She shook her head. "No. No, not at all. I was just overcome..."

With passion. With pleasure.

With love...

Luca didn't want to sleep. He didn't want to miss a minute of this magical evening with Aubrey—because he knew it wasn't going to last.

It couldn't.

Staying with her would put her in danger, too. Again. Still...

Today—in that barn—with all those shots fired, Aubrey could have been killed. He shuddered at the thought, and she murmured and shifted against his chest.

Her eyes opened, and she stared up at him. "I dozed off..."

"Shh, go back to sleep," he told her. He loved holding her like this, in his arms, her body warm and limp against his.

She shook her head.

And he knew she felt what he did—that she didn't want to waste their limited time together sleeping. He could sleep later when he was somewhere else and she was safe.

And when he did, he knew he would dream of her, of this night...

Of every kiss, of every caress, of every moment of pleasure...

It was only then that he would let himself also feel the pain, the loss of what could have been, had he been another man, had he not had a price on his head.

A knock at the door startled him, making him tense with fear. Had he messed up? Had he put her in danger by staying too long already?

"Room service," someone called out.

"You ordered dinner, remember?" Aubrey said. She must have felt his fear, too. But then her face flushed with embarrassment. "We got distracted after…"

When they'd been told how long it was going to take for their food to be done, they'd made good use of that time. Such good use that he had forgotten all about the food.

Another knock rattled the door.

"You better get that," she said. She slid out of the bed, scooped up her clothes from the floor and headed toward the bathroom, leaving him to answer the door.

He threw on his jeans and looked through the peephole before answering it. He didn't feel entirely safe. He wouldn't ever feel entirely safe again. That was just going to be the life he led from now on, one where he was constantly looking over his shoulder for the Camorra.

He opened the door and greeted the waiter who stood in the hall with a trolley of covered dishes. "Thank you." The kitchen had been about to close when he'd called, but they'd been happy to oblige them with one last meal.

That was how Luca felt. Like this was his last meal, his last day on earth.

His last moment of happiness.

He was here.

Paolo tensed as he heard his voice; he'd been coming back from the lobby bar when the door had opened to a room on the same hall as his. He hadn't even had to see Luca to know that it was him.

Thankfully, the waiter stood between Luca and the hall, so maybe his cousin hadn't seen him, either. He would be shocked if he had, and he would know exactly why Paolo was here.

To make sure that he was dead…

Whoever was shot at the Gemini ranch hadn't been Luca. Once again his cousin's luck had held, and he'd escaped again.

If the Camorra learned about this…

If Paolo didn't do something…

He didn't have his cousin's luck. He wouldn't escape death again and again.

If he didn't finish this—if he didn't finish off Luca—then the Camorra would finish him.

Chapter 23

Aubrey had ducked into the bathroom because she wasn't dressed. And because she'd needed a moment to compose herself...

Or she might have blurted out how she felt about Luca. That she'd fallen for him.

She didn't want this night to end. She didn't want him to leave. Ever.

But how could he stay?

His life would be in danger and hers would be as well, just as he'd warned her. Her heart ached already with missing him, and he hadn't left yet. She'd heard the deep rumble of his voice as he spoke with the waiter.

Then she'd heard the rattle of the food service cart as he wheeled it into the room. Even after she dressed and fixed her hair, which had been sticking up all over the place, she stood several long moments, waiting for the sound of the door closing behind the waiter, before she reached for the doorknob.

But when she tried turning it, it didn't budge. It was as if something was pinned beneath it.

"Luke?" she called out.

There was no reply.

"Luca?"

Had he left with the waiter?

She rattled the door, trying to dislodge whatever was pinned beneath it.

"Shh…" a deep voice murmured. "Stay in there and stay quiet."

"What—what's going on?" But she knew…even before he said it.

"You need to step back from the door," Luca said, his voice low and gruff with emotion.

"What—why?"

"Maybe climb into the bathtub or the shower…"

She glanced back at the walk-in shower. There was no bathtub. But she didn't want to step back from the door. Her hand gripped the knob even harder, but no matter how hard she tried, it wouldn't move.

"Luca…" Her heart was beating fast and heavy with fear. "What's going on?"

"It's going to all be over soon," he told her.

"What?" she asked, panic gripping her, stealing away her breath. "What's going to be over?"

Their magical evening? Their relationship? Or his life?

Luca hated doing this, but he had no choice. With the chair jammed beneath the knob to the bathroom door, she wasn't going to be able to get out. But some-one could still get inside…

Could still get to her.

This was a bad idea. All of it…

But there wasn't any time for a more elaborate plan. He'd only caught a glimpse of his cousin from the cor-ner of his eye, but he knew why he was here.

Paolo had to make sure the Camorra hitman had fin-ished the job, had finished Luca.

Even if Paolo hadn't seen him when he opened the door, he must have heard Luca talking to the waiter, and recognized his voice. Had he known Luca had checked into the hotel?

Or had it just been a cosmic coincidence that he'd registered at the same hotel? Fate…

Destiny that it was to end like this…

A knock rattled the door to the hallway. He drew in a breath to calm his nerves, and he reached up to check the buttons on his flannel shirt before heading toward the door. He forced a smile as he opened it, but that smile dropped along with his jaw as he feigned surprise at the person standing outside.

"Paolo!" he exclaimed. "I can't believe it's you. I thought it was the waiter." But he hadn't. He'd known his cousin was coming. That was why he'd shoved the chair under the bathroom doorknob. It was why he held his breath now, hoping that chair held.

"The waiter's gone," Paolo murmured, as he stepped inside the room and closed the door behind himself. "Just like you're supposed to be…"

He wasn't even going to make a pretense of why he was there, so Luca dropped his act as well and released a heavy sigh. "How long?" he asked. "How long have you been working for them?"

Paolo sighed, too. "A long time. I borrowed money for my business, for other things…"

Debts. Like Aubrey's ex-boyfriend, Paolo liked to gamble and must have had about as much luck at it as Warren Parker.

"I don't have a choice," Paolo said, and he pulled a gun from beneath the jacket he wore.

"Did they supply you with that weapon?" he asked.

Paolo shook his head. "Just with the money and connection to buy it from when I landed in Denver."

"They're setting you up," Luca warned him.

Paolo shrugged. "Probably. But either I do this, or I die, Luca. If I let you live, I'd be running just like you have been. And I don't have the luck you have, *cugino*. I won't be able to outrun them. So I have no choice."

"You do have a choice," Luca insisted. "You can go to the police. You can testify against whoever is pulling the strings now."

Because his cousin was so clearly just a puppet in the organization, a scapegoat they were setting up for Luca's murder.

"And then, after I testify, I would still wind up like you," Paolo said. "I would have to live like you're living, always on the run." He shuddered, probably imagining what that would be like.

"Always having to look over your shoulder, never being able to trust or get close to anyone…" Luca murmured with a weary sigh. "No, that's no way to live."

"Then maybe I'm doing you a favor," Paolo said. "I'm

putting you out of your misery." And he raised that gun and pointed the barrel at Luca.

Luca held up his hands. "Do *me* a favor," he implored his cousin.

Paolo shook his head. "I can't let you live," he said. "They will kill me for certain."

"Her…" He pointed toward the bathroom door. "Don't hurt her. She doesn't know who you are. She hasn't seen you. There's no reason to hurt her."

"I'm not sure the Camorra would see it that way," Paolo said. "You know how they say 'no witnesses.'"

Luca knew that all too well. It was why it had taken him so many years to compile information and evidence for the exposé. There had been very few people alive to talk to him, and the ones that had survived had only done so because they hadn't been willing to speak. It was probably also why the hitman had murdered the woman who'd posed as his wife. He hadn't wanted to leave behind a witness.

And the assassin had died without being able to testify or to negotiate a deal to offset some of his own prison time.

And now Luca was about to do the same, to lose his life forever.

"Please, Paolo," he implored his cousin. "Just leave her be. She has nothing to do with any of this."

She shouldn't have been with him. He knew that now. Knew that he'd put her at risk from the minute he'd checked into her ranch.

Paolo tilted his head as he studied Luca's face. "It's finally happened," he said. "You've finally fallen in love."

Luca couldn't deny it, but he couldn't declare it, either. It wouldn't be fair. Not to him and certainly not to Aubrey.

"Maybe you are human after all," Paolo remarked. "So maybe this will work this time…" He motioned with the gun. "Maybe when I pull this trigger, you will die."

Luca drew in a shaky breath, bracing himself. But he also needed to brace his cousin. "When you pull that trigger, it won't just be my life that's ending. Your life—as you know it—is over, too."

Tears brimmed in Paolo's dark eyes, and the barrel wavered as if he was choking. "I won't have a life if I don't do this. They will kill me."

"Paolo…"

His cousin shook his head. "I'm sorry, Luca. I'm so sorry…"

"I'm sorry, too," Luca said. He was sorry that he had to do this to Aubrey. But like Paolo, the Camorra had given him no choice. He would gladly give up his life for hers.

Hopefully, she would forgive him.

Paolo steadied his hand even as tears streaked down his face. Then he squeezed the trigger.

He must have had a silencer on the gun because the only thing Luca heard as he fell was the sound of Aubrey screaming.

He would have killed the woman, too. He'd raised the gun barrel toward the bathroom door, which was rattling from her pounding on it, when the door to the hall flew open.

"Drop the gun! Drop the gun!" a policeman yelled at him. A waiter stood next to him. He must have let the police into the room.

"You're too late," Paolo said, and his chest ached with disappointment. He glanced down at his cousin lying so still on the floor. "You're too late. He's dead."

And the woman, locked inside the bathroom, screamed even louder.

Chapter 24

A couple of weeks had passed since that horrible night in the hotel. Since the night Aubrey had lost Luca forever…

She'd known he was going to leave. But she'd thought he was going to walk away from her, not be wheeled out of their room in a body bag. She'd hoped that wherever he lived, he'd live a full life, traveling, writing, smiling.

But he could do none of those things now. And Aubrey was barely able to make herself do anything, either. But she had the ranch and responsibilities. She couldn't let down her twin and the rest of her family. And most of all, she couldn't let down Luca's memory. He'd been so convinced that she was strong. So she needed to prove that she was—to him and, most of all, to herself.

So an hour earlier, she had walked into her mother's house with a smile on her face, intent on assuring everyone that she was fine. And she'd held on to that smile during their impromptu meeting of the Truth Foundation, so that every time someone looked at her—and they'd looked often—she'd appeared to be happy.

"Fake it until you make it," her mother remarked as she joined Aubrey in the kitchen.

In order to get away from the intent gazes of her family, Aubrey had started to clear the cups and glasses out of the family room that adjoined the kitchen. Not everyone had showed up, but with her family being as busy and far-flung as they were, it was rare for everybody to show up for a meeting. Morgan, Caleb and Nadine were here. And Gideon had showed up as well, along with their sister Rachel and her adorable baby girl, Iris. Seeing Iris usually made Aubrey happy, but today she'd just been reminded that she wouldn't be able to have one of her own with the man she'd wanted to spend her life with.

Who was the father of Rachel's baby? Her sister had never said, and with her busy career as the district attorney, she never seemed to have time to date. Maybe she'd just decided to become a mother on her own; that was what Aubrey would do, too, if she wanted children but never fell in love again.

In the family room, the meeting was still going on, Caleb assuring everyone that his and Morgan's amazing assistant, Rebekah, was on Ronald Spence's case. If anyone could find the evidence to indicate whether or not Spence was actually innocent, she would. Aubrey had wondered from the beginning if there was anything to be found.

"What do you mean about faking it?" Aubrey asked her mother. "Do you have doubts about Spence's claims of innocence, too?"

Her mother smiled and shook her head, and her blond hair swept across her shoulders. "I have doubts about you," her mother said. "I don't think you're doing as well as you want everyone to believe you're doing."

Aubrey tried to force a smile, but hard as she tried, she couldn't pull up the corners of her mouth. She was just too tired and filled with grief.

Her mom pulled Aubrey's hand away from the cups on the counter and squeezed it. "I could always tell when you were putting on a brave face, Aubrey. You don't need to do that with me. I can tell you're hurting." And she closed her arms around her, pulling her into a warm hug.

For a moment Aubrey gave in to the comfort and let herself relax in her mom's arms. She even let her head settle on Isa Colton's strong shoulder. But then tears stung her eyes, and she knew that if she gave in to them, she wouldn't stop crying.

She inhaled shakily and pulled back. "I'll be okay," she assured her mom.

"I wish I had had the chance to meet him," her mother said. "Sounds like Luca Rossi was quite a guy and very smart."

Aubrey nodded. "He was. His exposés were amazing. So thorough that he took down entire organizations." And then they'd taken him down, using his own cousin to carry out the crime.

"I know that he was smart because he cared about you," her mother said. "He was smart to realize what an amazing woman you are."

Aubrey smiled—for real now. "Yes, I am. I get it from my mama."

Isa chuckled. "Yes, you do," she agreed. "I know all about faking that you're okay until you actually are." She squeezed Aubrey's shoulder. "You will be. Eventually."

She wanted to ask how long it took, how long she would have this hollow ache inside her before she finally started feeling whole again. Genuinely happy again. Because right now she couldn't see it; she couldn't see that far into the future.

All she could see was that image of the body bag with Luca zipped up inside it. Every time she closed her eyes, it flashed through her mind. And even now, with her eyes open, it appeared to her again. Now she closed her eyes and tried to shut it out. Tried to forget…

But she would never be able to forget that horrific night. She would never be able to forget Luca, either.

"Did you forget?" Jasper asked.

Aubrey felt a sickening lurch in her stomach and opened her eyes, shocked at her twin's question and at his sudden appearance. She'd thought she was alone with her mother in the kitchen. Jasper must have slipped out of the meeting in the family room as well.

"Forget what?" she asked him. Unlike her and their mother, he wasn't carrying dishes. He just held the keys to the ranch truck, jangling them as they dangled from his fingers.

"Did you forget that I wanted you to meet with the applicant for a ranch hand?" he asked.

Until he'd mentioned it on the drive to their mother's house, Aubrey hadn't even realized that he'd advertised for a new employee. She could understand why he thought they needed one now—to pick up her slack.

With her tossing and turning all night, she didn't have much energy to pull her weight during the day— even though she wanted to throw herself into work. Into anything that would take her mind off Luca.

But not this…

Interviewing a new ranch hand, training them, would remind her entirely too much of Luca—how he'd helped move the cattle like a ranch hand, and taken care of the calf.

Tears stung her eyes again, but she blinked them back. "I think you can handle an interview on your own," she told her partner.

He shook his head. "No. We need to both be able to get along with him. He needs to be a good fit for the business and for the family."

"It's just a minor position," she reminded her twin. "The guy's not going to become part of the Colton clan."

Jasper laughed. "You never know…"

"Are you going to marry him?" she asked.

"Let's interview him first," Jasper said. "And we'll see where it goes from there."

She laughed, too, at her brother's teasing. He'd been working really hard to keep her mind off Luca, off her loss.

"It would be lovely," their mother said, "to have more weddings and babies in this family, more happy events."

Aubrey couldn't deny that it would be good. She just knew she wasn't going to be the one personally having any of those special events.

She sighed. "Okay, Jasper, let's go interview your future spouse."

She hugged her mother again and then moved on to her other relatives remaining in the family room, assuring them all that she would be okay. Gideon tilted his head, though, and studied her face with skepticism and sympathy.

He hugged her again and murmured in her ear. "It'll take time, but you'll be okay."

She nodded. "I know." But how did Gideon know?

"Be patient with yourself, Aubrey," he encouraged her.

She nodded again and pulled back. "Now, we better get going," she urged Jasper. She wanted the hell out of there before her siblings offered any more comfort—it would just make her fall apart.

And she could not do that. Not now, not ever. She had to be strong like their mother had been strong when their father died. At least Luca hadn't died like Ben Colton—in disgrace. He'd died a hero, making certain to keep her safe.

Isa Colton had focused on her family after her husband died. Aubrey had ranch business to focus on, and when, less than an hour later, she and Jasper were back at the ranch, she breathed a slight sigh of relief.

Instead of stopping at the main lodge, Jasper drove the pickup past it. "Where are you going?" she asked.

"The barn," he said. "You can't hire a ranch hand if he doesn't know anything about horses or cattle."

"Surely you looked over his application and verified his work history and references," she said.

"We didn't do that last time," Jasper said, "with Luke Bishop, even though he didn't work for us."

She gasped as a deep pain stabbed her heart at the mention of Luca.

"Sorry," he said sincerely. He pulled the truck up outside the barn and braked. "I'm also sorry that I forgot that application and those references. Why don't you go meet him—he's waiting for you in the tack room—and I'll grab that stuff and be right back?"

Aubrey furrowed her brow and studied her twin's face. "What are you up to?" He couldn't seriously be trying to play matchmaker between her and some ranch hand applicant.

And that pang struck her again. The past couple of weeks Jasper had been so supportive and sensitive; he hadn't even mentioned Luke's name. And now...

"What is up with you?" she asked. Had it all been too much for him? Was he sick of having to do all the ranch work with her being so distracted and upset? "What's going on?"

He shook his head. "Nothing. Just go into the barn and meet the applicant. I'll be right back with his paperwork."

She hesitated a long moment before she reached for the door handle; she wasn't sure she was ready for this. Hanging out with her family at the Truth Foundation meeting at Mom's had been hard enough. Interviewing a stranger for a position she would have liked Luke Bishop to keep...

It bordered on cruel.

Not that Luke Bishop had been real, and Luca Rossi had been no ranch hand. If only…

She exhaled a sigh and opened the door. She'd barely closed it before Jasper was backing up and driving off. Maybe he was just in a hurry to retrieve that paperwork, or maybe he was in a hurry to get away from her.

Had she been that difficult to be around the past two weeks? Maybe he'd been sensing all her pain. She couldn't blame him for wanting a break from that.

She wanted a break from that, so maybe interviewing this job applicant would be a welcome distraction. She forced herself to open the side door of the barn and step inside. She'd only visited the barn a couple of times over the past two weeks. It had been hard to be in here and not think about that day—about the man trying to kill Luca. She'd saved him then.

Maybe if he hadn't locked her in the bathroom, she could have kept him alive that night in the hotel. But he hadn't given her the chance. He'd been trying to protect her.

She knew that and she loved him for it.

So she forced herself to walk to the tack room. This was another place where she had too many memories of Luca, of making love with him for the first time…

Her hand trembled slightly as she closed it around the doorknob and opened the door. The ranch hand applicant didn't turn around; he stood with his back to her. Wearing faded jeans and cowboy boots and a cowboy hat, he was tall and lean and so achingly familiar.

Was she imagining Luca here again…with her?

Then he turned, and shock staggered her, knocking her back a couple of feet. He reached for her, catching her shoulders in his hands as if he was worried that she was going to faint.

He'd told her that he was an only child, so he had no twin. Unless he'd lied about that.

Unless he hadn't died, he couldn't be here. He couldn't be here. But when she raised her hands to his face, he felt real. Her skin tingled from the contact with his salt-and-pepper stubble.

This was Luca.

Alive and well.

"How?" she asked. But even as she asked it, she knew. He'd locked her in that bathroom and nobody had let her out until the suspect had been taken from the room, until the body had been zipped into that bag. She hadn't even been able to see him one last time before they wheeled him off.

Two weeks away from her had been interminably long. And Luca had known that she was alive and well. He'd just missed her—so much that he tried to reach out now. But she stepped back, and her hands fell away from his face.

Behind the lenses of her glasses, her eyes were still wide with shock. But also with knowledge…

She must have realized how he'd pulled it off. But did she understand why?

"I'm sorry," he said.

"For what?" she asked. "Sorry that you let me believe you were dead or sorry that you're alive?"

"I wouldn't blame you for being furious with me," he said. "I know how much it means to you to always know the truth, no secrets, no lies…"

"And still you fooled me anyway," she murmured.

His heart ached for the pain in her voice and on her beautiful face, and regret filled him that he'd hurt her. That was the last thing he'd wanted to do.

"I'm sorry," he said again. "I wasn't trying to fool you. I was trying to fool my cousin and the Camorra. And to protect you from both."

Would she understand that? Could she?

He went back to her first question now. "When room service came, the waiter was someone you know—Dominic."

She gasped. "Dominic was in on this?"

He nodded. "He put the chair beneath the bathroom door."

The FBI agent had been as determined to protect his sister as Luca had been.

"After he heard about what happened at the ranch with the assassin, he came to the hotel to provide us with protection. He heard someone mention the Italian guy who'd checked in earlier. He was worried that he was another hitman sent after me, and he came to warn me. He outfitted me with a bulletproof vest—just in time."

"So you weren't shot?" she asked.

He flinched and touched his ribs. "I was shot, but the vest stopped the bullet." Just not the force of it that had cracked some bones. But he would share that with her later, if she would give him another chance.

"And you and my brother let me believe you were dead this whole time?" she asked, her voice low with anger.

"We couldn't tell you the truth," he said. "You had

to appear upset—in case any of your other guests were working for the Camorra."

She shivered as if she hadn't considered that there could have been more. The thought had haunted him, just as her screams had plagued him the past two weeks.

"We had to wait until everyone here at that time had checked out before we could tell you the truth. I couldn't risk someone hurting you to get to me," he said.

Her lips parted, as if she was about to say something. He could imagine what, so he continued, "I know that I hurt you, and if you'll give me the chance, I'd like to spend the rest of my life making it up to you."

Now her brow furrowed with confusion. "But... how...?"

"The Camorra think I'm dead," he said. And only his mother knew the truth. "We convinced Paolo of that by letting him shoot me and then the authorities declaring me dead and zipping me into that body bag." He shuddered as he remembered that feeling, one he never wanted to experience again. "They're not going to come after me anymore. In order to stay out of jail and going into witness protection, Paolo agreed to testify against everybody he knew that was left in the organization. The FBI has checked their international intel, and they don't think anyone's free to come after me. And everyone in jail believes I'm dead. I can stay here without putting you in danger. And I'd like to stay—if you want me...like I want you..." He stepped closer to her then and slid his arms around her waist. "So very much..."

"What will I call you?" she asked.

He shrugged. "It doesn't matter."

"But what name will you use here?" she asked.

"I've kept the Luke Bishop credentials," he said. "That'll work. But you can call me Luca. Or better yet, husband."

Her eyes widened. "Are you proposing?"

He nodded. "I know that I've hurt you, and that I will have to work to earn back your trust before you would consider accepting my proposal, but I love you, Aubrey Colton. I can't imagine my life without you. Please, at least consider giving me another chance."

She flung her arms around him then and pulled his head down toward hers. As her lips brushed across his, she murmured. "You have it."

He pulled back just slightly to ask, "What do I have?"

"A second chance," she said. "And my love and my trust. I love you, Luca."

His mother's hands were elbow-deep in soapy water in the kitchen sink when the phone rang, so Gideon answered it.

"Colton residence," he said.

"Gideon!" Aubrey exclaimed, her voice vibrating with excitement.

At least he thought it was Aubrey; she certainly hadn't sounded like this when she'd been here earlier. And even though she'd pasted a smile on her face, it had been painfully forced. "Is everything all right?" he asked her.

"It's perfect," she said. "Please bring Mom out to the ranch. Get everybody out here as soon as possible."

"Why? What's going on?" he asked.

And Mom, wiping her hands on a dish towel, repeated his question. "What's going on? Who is that?"

"Tell Mom that she can meet him—thanks to Dominic. All of you can meet him."

"Who?"

"Luca Rossi."

"I thought he was dead."

"He was. I guess he is, but Luke Bishop is alive and no longer has a hit out on him. He's here at the ranch with me. And I want you all to meet him. I want you to meet the man that I love."

Tears sprang to Gideon's eyes. He'd never heard Aubrey so happy. And while he was thrilled for her—that she would be able to be with the person she loved, he felt a pang of envy as well.

Gideon had been in love once.

Probably still was…

But unlike Aubrey, that person hadn't loved him back. He forced that thought from his mind, though, and focused on his sister's happiness. She deserved it, and it sounded as though she'd finally found it.

* * * * *

*Don't miss the first book in the
miniseries,*
Colton's Pursuit of Justice, *by Marie Ferrarella.
Available now from Harlequin Romantic Suspense!*

And don't miss the next volume,
Colton's Dangerous Reunion, *by Justine Davis,
available next month.*

#2175 COLTON'S DANGEROUS REUNION
The Coltons of Colorado • by Justine Davis

When social worker Gideon Colton reports a parent for child abuse, he never thought he'd put his ex—the child's pediatrician—in harm's way. Now he and Sophie Gray-Jones are thrown back together to avoid danger...and find themselves reigniting the flame that never really went out.

#2176 FINDING THE RANCHER'S SON
by Karen Whiddon

Jackie Burkholdt's sister and nephew are missing, so she returns home to their tiny West Texas hometown. The boy's father, Eli Pitts, might be the most obvious suspect, but he and Jackie are helplessly drawn to each other. As secrets come to light, it becomes even harder to know who is responsible—let alone who it's safe to have feelings for.

#2177 BODYGUARD UNDER SIEGE
Bachelor Bodyguards • by Lisa Childs

Keeli Abbott became a bodyguard to *avoid* Detective Spencer Dubridge. Now she's been tasked with protecting him—and might be pregnant with his baby! Close quarters force them to face their feelings, but with a drug cartel determined to make sure Spencer doesn't testify, they may not have much time left...

#2178 MOUNTAIN RETREAT MURDER
Cameron Glen • by Beth Cornelison

When a mysterious death finds Cait Cameron's family's inn, she enlists guest Matt Harkney, father to a troubled teenager, to help investigate recent crimes. Love and loyalty are tested as veteran Matt risks everything to heal his family, catch a thief and save Cait's life.

SPECIAL EXCERPT FROM

Ⓗ HARLEQUIN

ROMANTIC SUSPENSE

When a mysterious death finds Cait Cameron's family's inn, she enlists guest Matt Harkney, father to a troubled teenager, to help investigate recent crimes. Love and loyalty are tested as veteran Matt risks everything to heal his family, catch a thief and save Cait's life.

Read on for a sneak preview of
Mountain Retreat Murder,
*the first book in Beth Cornelison's
new Cameron Glen miniseries!*

He paused with the blade hovering over the crack between boards. "Are you sure you want to keep prying up planks? Whoever did this could have loosened any number of boards in this floor."

The truth of his comment clearly daunted her. Her shoulders dropped, and her expression sagged with sorrow. "Yes. Continue. At least with this one, where I know something was amiss earlier." She raised a hand, adding, "But carefully."

He ducked his head in understanding, "Of course."

An apologetic grin flickered over her forlorn features, softening the tension, and he took an extra second or two just to stare at her. Sunlight streamed in from the window above the kitchen sink and highlighted the auburn streaks in her hair and the faint freckles on her upturned nose. The bright beam reflected in her pale blue eyes, reminding him of sparkling water in the stream by his cabin. A throb of emotion grabbed at his chest.

"Matt?"

"Do you know how beautiful you are?"

She blinked. Blushed.

"What?" The word sounded strangled.

"You are." He stroked her cheek with the back of his left hand. "Beautiful."

Her throat worked as she swallowed, and she glanced down, shyly. "Um, thank you. I—"

"Anyway…" He withdrew his hand and turned his attention back to the floorboard. He eased the pocketknife blade in the small crack and gently levered the plank up.

As he moved the board out of the way, Cait shined the flashlight in the hole beneath.

She gasped at the same moment he muttered, "Holy hell."

In the dark space they exposed was a small plastic bag. Cait moved the light closer, illuminating the contents of the clear bag—a large bundle of cash, bound by a white paper band with "$7458" written on it.

When she reached for the bag of money, he caught her wrist. "No. Don't touch it."

When she frowned a query at him, he added, "Fingerprints. That's evidence."

Don't miss
Mountain Retreat Murder *by Beth Cornelison,*
available April 2022 wherever
Harlequin Romantic Suspense
books and ebooks are sold.

Harlequin.com

HRSEXP0222